CHIRON review

ISSUE #133, SUMMER 2024

ST. JOHN, KANSAS

CHIRON review

Issue #133, SUMMER 2024

Poetry Editors
Wendy Rainey, Clint Margrave, Grant Hier, Sarah Daugherty

Fiction Editors
Rafael Zepeda, Sarah Daugherty, Dave Newman

Art/Design Director: Craig Ashby

Cover photo: Buster Keaton, 1925, Library of Congress

Chiron Review is indexed by *Humanities International Complete*. Issues 18-81 were indexed by *Index of American Periodical of Verse*. *CR* is microfilmed by ProQuest, Ann Arbor, MI. Its archive is housed at Beinecke Rare Book & Manuscript Library, Yale University, New Haven, CT; Princeton University Library, Princeton, NJ; Temple University Library, Philadelphia; and Kenneth Spencer Research Library, University of Kansas, Lawrence.

Opinions expressed by the writers and artists in this journal are their own and not to be considered those of the publisher or the editors.

ISSN: 1046-8897

ISBN: 978-1-304-33754-2

Michael Hathaway, Publisher
chironreview2@gmail.com

❧ *Author Index* ❧

Redux: Mississippi Delta

A late day in August, and your secondhand Buick
    carries you east of Hushpuckena til the compass

leans toward Clarksdale. A bluesman's
    Stratocaster holds sway amid verdant farms.

Hot winds shuffle jewelweed and mallow
    like the fluttering eyelids of dreamy children.

How long have you waited for this?
    Soon, you'll face your daughter,

pregnant again with your fourth grandchild
    from a man you've never met.

As you take an exit that fades to gravel
    and switchgrass – the road's name forgettable,

a hawk drops through the sun.
    Its wings angle hard in the failing light.

JC Alfier

With Our Eyes Half-Closed in a Bayou Town

Always trust neon shaped to any doorway.
Trust legs crossed in nylon trying hard to evade

splinters on a porch's wooden bench, headlights
sweeping the boozy eyes of everyone who sits there –

booze we know we'll never sweat out.
Gravel and blood are chips off the old block,

kids pacing in the footfalls of betters
they know were never better, backhanded grins glowing.

Possession is nine-tenths of everything here,
the windfall of theft – petty or grand.

Though we'll never wipe the evidence clean,
we try to be someone gone who was never here.

We're shadows in each other's eyes
and you know what goes down when we resist

what'll never change, like sermons that go on too long,
like a fugitive chancing down our streets,

summer sun he once loved in a place like ours,
a place offering him nothing but thirst,

the fecund black soil of wherever
he calls home beguiling him headlong,

like a divorcee shushed by her child
for singing late into evening, her mind's eye

packing everything she owns, her lipstick
so bright it could trample darkness right out of the room.

JC Alfier

Post-Storm Cerulean Blue
– for Chris

How heavily he danced
with his chainsaw
in the upper branches
of a beechwood –
slow lunge and quick step,
greenstick bend
and leaf shimmer.
"When the bough breaks ..."
the nursery rhyme warns
but he did not fall, not then.
Under an impossibly blue sky
we set fire to the tree debris
and watched the flames itch
for heaven. Never mind
the powerlines
or sizzle and pop
of young burning wood.

Jen Ashburn

First Love

He says he's not a nice guy   & maybe that's true
but I still knock   on his trailer door   that first Saturday night after
that first kiss   the one that shimmied & teased   until we couldn't help
but fall into it   I wanna fall   some more   He invites me in
We watch *Star Trek: The Next Generation*   talk about the pizza place
where we both work   while his fish tanks glow fluorescent blue
against cuts of TV light   the aerators gurgling under
"Set phasers to stun"   & Jean-Luc Picard's   smooth-tongued
"Make it so"

       Oh, the world he's created for these fish
the discus & neon tetras   the angel fish & plecostomus
the care he's taken to get the water   just right
Even then I know   the water's not right   for us   but my body's
handkerchief   crumples   to his sweaty palm
& I will go   anywhere   in his breast pocket
He leads me to a bedroom   with yet another fish tank –
discus he's trying to breed   hundreds of eggs on a rock slab
"It's not like the movies," he says   as he pulls off my T-shirt
but I don't believe him because we are   after all   in the movie
of my life   & there is so much to discover   We are inelegant
animals   naked on a raw mattress   bathed in skittering light.

Jen Ashburn

The Edge of Twilight

At the edge of twilight
I walk out the door,
all my life drawn to be
present in the light I feel going.
It isn't the sunset
warm colors calling,
or anything eyes can see.
It's my whole body knowing
now is the time to be
leaning on the doorpost
with nothing to accomplish,
or walking the hills,
not to get somewhere
but to be in the presence
of what I can't name,
alive in my body
on this body Earth,
to feel in the changing light
the dark coming.

Mary Isabel Azrael

The Young Mother

My mother tells me a story
– not a story –
a few treasured facts
of my life before I was
in it on my own.
I lean closer to hear
things that happened to her
when she and I were one.
How I thrill to the words
where you were conceived
in the house full of clocks and dinosaur bones,
a stranger's house in a strange landscape
in the middle of Texas in the middle of the war.
1943. Nobody knew how it would end.
Sixty-two years ago,
and now she's beginning to say
There's not much time.
I always thought there was plenty of time
but there isn't.

We sit, our arms touching, at the seder table
with everyone talking around us disappearing,
and inside me the young mother she was
stretches out at the foot of my bed
leaning on her elbow,
telling the little girl I was
stories of the adventure she lived
before I was born,
when she and I were one.

Mary Isabel Azrael

A.R. Bender

Right Next Time

All the months of traveling had worn him out, but he didn't want the journey to end yet either.

He stared out the airplane window, still mildly intoxicated by the last of his Lomotil prescription. The jumbled pattern of towns and roads outside LA had now given way to an arid landscape where a single wide freeway, Interstate 10, extended far to the east. Directly south, he recognized the indigo-blue shape of the Salton Sea, which stood out so prominently from the surrounding rugged brown terrain. He last saw it seven months earlier when flying from Phoenix to LA; the first leg of what he hoped to be a journey of self-discovery. But the trip hadn't turned out the way he expected and now he was returning to the place where it all began.

Seven months: he thought the forty grand he won on that lucky day at the Golden Gate Fields racetrack would've lasted a little longer. At least he had enough left – about eight thousand by his last count – to drive along those Route 66 roads for a while. Or maybe he'd push on to New Orleans, where he had so much fun during the Mardi Gras the year before. Hell, he was too wasted to figure that out yet. As the airplane descended through a layer of clouds to the airport, he mused about all the places he's been to in South America, the Caribbean, and Mexico.

Sky Harbor; what a perfect name for an airport. Or so he thought at the time. When he departed, the name conjured images of being on a boat heading towards exotic South Seas destinations in search of buried treasure. Now it was like coming back with an empty haul.

James was waiting by the baggage check and couldn't disguise an expression of disbelief when he approached him with his luggage.

"Wow, Ray. I hardly recognized you," James said, extending his arms out in an embrace. "That hair. And tan. Have you lost weight or something?"

"The food poisoning in San Blas did me in but I'm better now. How's Sylvia?"

"Finished another sculpture. She just got a job in a ritzy art gallery."

"Good for her. What about you?"

"Same old same old. Still at the insurance company."

"Did you bring the Alfa?"

"Sure did. I've taken it out a couple times a week like you said but not too far. It's tough to drive around here without air conditioning."

Ray felt a pleasant burst of recognition when he spotted his dark green '72 Alfa Romeo GTV 2000 parked in the corner of the airport garage. He bought it two years before, in 1986, because of the low miles and cherry body. The engine idled a little rough, so he pulled back the choke cable handle a bit to smooth out revs.

"You have to tell us about the trip during dinner tonight," James said. "We only got a couple of postcards from you."

"I've been in some pretty remote places and sometimes lost track of things." He chuckled. "Like time and place."

"Ha! Sounds like the time we watched the sunset on top of Mount Tamalpais on acid."

"No acid this time. I met some Brits in Rio and followed them to a commune up the coast near Salvador. I hung out there for over two months, I think, getting buzzed on mescaline and weed. Hooking up with women from almost every Euro nationality. But I split when the cops started busting people for the drugs and stuff."

"Same old Ray. Pushing the envelope."

He backed out of the parking slot and squealed the tires as he drove off.

They were halfway back to their place in Chandler when he finished telling James about his affair in Buenos Aires with Gabriella, and how he burned through almost eight grand with her in a little over a month; going to expensive nightclubs, discos, restaurants, and casinos.

"That's a lot of coin. Was she worth it?"

"Absolutely. There's something about Argentine women. They look and act more European than Latin. In fact, most Argentines do. I left when she started fishing for stuff like cars and jewelry."

"Speaking of hot women," James said, "Zena visited us last week. Remember her?"

Her name jolted him out of his travel reverie. "Of course. You still keep in touch with her?"

"Sylvia has been. She's come by a few times to visit since she settled in Taos last year."

"What's she doing there?"

"Running an art workshop. She moved there to be closer to her Navajo relatives."

"She has Native blood?"

"On her mother's side, Sylvia said. She made us a beautiful Dream Catcher artifact. And another gift for you called a Medicine Wheel."

"Too bad she couldn't have stayed a few more days."

"She left to teach some classes there. We all thought you'd be here by then based on your last card from Puerto Vallarta."

"I should've stayed there and not gone up to goddamn San Blas. I never got sick during the whole trip. And then puke my guts out from the bad fish at the end."

Ray thought about Zena the rest of the drive back. She'd been part of the crowd he hung around with during his college years in Berkeley. He'd always been attracted to her but didn't pursue it because he was going out with Kirsten at the time. The few times when they talked alone together Zena always seemed genuinely interested in his musical career. Like the time she asked him if he ever considered composing his own music. The question lingered with him for a long time until he decided to give it a shot during the trip.

The three of them had just finished dinner, talking about old times and Ray's journey. Sylvia poured them more wine and walked over to the stereo.

"Here's some music you might like," she said to Ray.

After she popped in the cassette, he recognized it right away.

"La Dolce Vita."

"A soundtrack of Fellini movies," she said.

"Does this remind you of anything?" James asked.

"Sure does," he answered, taken in by a haunting solo trumpet passage in the Nino Rota score.

"The all-night Fellini Film Festival at the Bogart Theater," James said. "Just the four of us."

"Just the four of us," Ray answered with downcast eyes, recalling the days with Kirsten when they all lived together in an old Victorian house near the Berkeley Hills.

James and Sylvia exchanged concerned glances.

"Sounds like you had some amazing adventures," Sylvia said in an upbeat tone. "Did you do any composing?"

"Not much."

"Huh?" James said. "I thought that was the main reason for the trip. Find a place, rent a piano, and write some music."

"Well, I guess that didn't fucking work out!" he blurted out. He took note of their startled expressions. "Sorry. I must be tired."

"You do look a little ragged," James said.

"I think those meds messed up my sleep patterns." He took another sip of wine. "Anyway, I made plans to settle near Rio for the music until those Brits came along. Then I couldn't get back into it. So I told myself to enjoy the rest of the trip and do some composing later."

"Are you going back to the Bay Area now?" Sylvia asked.

"I don't know," Ray answered.

"You don't seem too thrilled about it," Sylvia said.

"I'm not. The thought depresses me. It's like I can't return unless I have something to show from the trip."

"Think you can get back with the orchestra?" James asked.

"Doubtful. I didn't exactly leave on good terms. Don't want to anyway. I was getting burned out on it all." He gazed out the window. "Taking those damn piano lessons since childhood. The recitals. More lessons and recitals. The music degree. The job at the orchestra. That's what it became to me – a job." He shook his head. "I thought the money I'd won at the track was like an act of destiny or something. So I could compose stuff I really like."

"You'll find a place for that," Sylvia said. "When you do, maybe you'll find someone special to be with. Instead of being alone."

"Where do you plan to go now?" James asked.

"New Orleans. I went to the Mardi Gras last year and made a few friends I'd like to see again. Plus, something about the town grabbed me. Especially the music scene."

"You should visit Zena on your way," Sylvia said. "Let me show you the gift she made for you."

She returned from the next room holding a flat box. He opened it and picked up a colorful hoop about eight inches in diameter. Four evenly spaced sticks radiated out from a central whitish object to the edge of the hoop. Thin strips of different colored leather were wrapped around each quadrant.

"Interesting. So this is a Medicine Wheel."

"She whipped out all these materials out of a bag of stuff and put it all together," James said. "It was cool to watch."

"She explained what it means," Sylvia said. "Something about how each color represents a different direction. Let's see. The white is north, west is red, black is south, and yellow is east. She also said that a person can't fully understand the meaning of life until they travel in all four directions."

"What's this object in the middle?" Ray asked, as he touched it with his index finger.

"She said it's a bone fragment from a buffalo skull," she answered.

He stared intently at the fragment. Something about it evoked a memory he couldn't quite recall.

"You guys would make a great couple," James slurred. He took another swig of wine. "You'd fit right in to where she's living now. For sure, you two oughta get together."

Ray tossed and turned on a couch in Sylvia's workshop, unable to sleep. He stretched out and stared at the sculptures she created, most of them in animal and humanoid form, silhouetted against the moonlight on a shelf in front of a window. After a while he got a creepy feeling that the statues were staring at *him*. He switched on a table lamp and reached for a magazine, but shifted his attention to the Medicine Wheel next to it. Once again, he was drawn to the circular bone fragment. The little craters and ridges on the convex surface reminded him of pictures of the moon ... like the lustrous full moon shining through his bedroom window when convalescing in San Blas. Just then, the elusive memory he had about the fragment earlier in the evening came back to him.

During one of those feverish nights in San Blas, he had a Lomotil-induced vision about strolling along a quiet, sandy beach near the end of a day toward a rising moon on the far horizon ... *a slender silhouette of a woman appeared against the moon farther down the beach walking toward him. When she got closer he sensed he knew her, but when he reached out to touch her the image dissolved before his eyes ...*

He flopped back down on the couch and imagined that the woman in this vision was Zena. He recalled the times they talked together back in the Berkeley days and especially her pensive, penetrating gaze – as if searching for something deep within his soul and spirit.

He spent the next week at their place fattening up on Sylvia's cooking and getting his sleep patterns back in sync. They both worked during the day so he had the house to himself. One day he drove to Phoenix, where he bought Sylvia a cassette of Chopin music, her favorite composer, and a fifth of Maker's Mark, James' favorite whiskey. There, he got a much-needed haircut and beard trim.

He'd known them for almost five years, ever since he and Kirsten were going out together in college. James and Sylvia married a year after they graduated. He and Kirsten talked about marriage too – until the Multiple Sclerosis hit her. He helped care for her at first, but the disease progressed so fast that her parents in Seattle took her back. She passed away six months later. Her death hit him hardest at the funeral. He couldn't get through his words during the ceremony without choking up. They were like soulmates.

After that, things started going sideways for him: losing his interest and passion for music; slipping into drug and gambling habits; chasing the wrong women in the wrong places. Like Gabriela. The type he knew wouldn't last but found almost irresistible. And hell – he had to admit it – the real reason he wanted to go to New Orleans: to hook up with the women he met in the Mardi Gras. Like Carlee, that sultry Cajun artist who lived in a converted art studio on Magazine Street.

But Zena was different. More like Kirsten. Now he had a chance to meet her again.

Ray was browsing through one of Sylvia's art books when James came in with a briefcase in hand.

"Home early huh," Ray said.

"Had a doctor's appointment and took the rest of the day off."

James brought out a six-pack of beer from the fridge. They both cracked open a can.

"You look healthier now," James said. "Not like such a wild man anymore."

"Sylvia's cooking got my strength back up."

"We're having Mahi-Mahi tonight."

"You guys have been too much. Taking care of my car and now this."

"We like having you over. Reminds us of the good times we had in Berkeley."

"To the good times in Berkeley," Ray repeated raising his beer in a toast.

"I've got to confess that I kind of admire you," James said. "Traveling to all those places. We've been talking about going to the Yucatan or Baja soon."

"I have a confession to make too. Traveling ain't all what you think. It was great at first, but after Brazil, things began to change." He took a swig of beer. "Maybe I'd been on the road too long, but in the last few months I got this weird feeling like something was chasing me. So I pushed myself to go to another place to get away. Sometimes I forgot where I was when I woke up in the morning. One day I hopped on a boat and ended up on some Caribbean island. Martinique. I've no idea how I got to Belize. Machu Picchu seems like an otherworldly dream. Like I was never there."

"Crazy. Sounds like one of my childhood nightmares. Something chasing me. My feet getting heavy. Slowing me down. As *it* was coming closer." He popped open another can. "So you're on the road again tomorrow."

"Yup. Ready to roll."

"I think you ought to take Sylvia's advice and visit Zena first."

"I haven't decided yet."

"You should, man. Trust me on this. There's something regal and goddess-like about her. To tell you the truth, I think she took the trip after Sylvia told her you'd be here."

16

He tried to figure out where to go first before he went to sleep. Taos made the most sense. From what James had said, it sounded like Zena was open to seeing him again. If things worked out between them, he could stay and compose music. And in what better place: a refuge for so many writers and artists since the time of D.H. Lawrence. On the other hand, he couldn't get his mind off the allure of hooking up with the women he met in New Orleans.

The next morning, Sylvia fixed a sumptuous breakfast that he washed down with plenty of strong coffee. He patted his stomach after he took the last bite of hash browns.

"All fueled up for the road."

"We're going to miss you," she said. "Thanks again for the Chopin music. We'll think about you whenever we play it."

"And I'll think about you whenever I guzzle down the Maker's," James said.

James helped him pack his luggage in the trunk of the Alfa.

He turned and embraced Sylvia. She handed him a folded-up piece of paper.

"Zena's address and phone number," she said. "Take care and drive carefully."

"Keep in touch man," James said, as they shook hands.

Ray waved to them as he drove away. They held each other's hands as they waved back. It almost made him think that getting hitched wasn't such a bad idea.

He stared at the I-10 freeway signs as he fueled up on the outskirts of Chandler. On one side of the road, a sign pointed to the northbound entrance. Across the street, another sign pointed south. Inside the Alfa, he studied the Rand McNally roadmap. To Taos, he'd head north on I-10, take I-70 to Flagstaff and from there follow those old Route 66 roads east through Gallup and Albuquerque towards Santa Fe. To New Orleans, he'd follow I-10 south to Tucson and east across Texas to Louisiana. He stared out at the signs for some time, unable to decide. Then he noticed something on the map that gave him a reprieve. Along I-10 at Las Cruces, I-25 branched off and headed directly north past Truth or Consequences and Albuquerque toward Taos. What a relief. Now he wouldn't have to decide until he came to Las Cruces.

Once on the southbound freeway, he listened to an alternative radio station that played songs like "Whip It" and "Addicted to Love." The sexy MTV videos of both made him fantasize about all the temptations waiting for him in New Orleans. Later, he popped in a cassette of *A Kind Of Blue*. The sound and rhythm of the piano and muted Miles Davis trumpet fit perfectly with his mood for traveling on the open road. He liked this mode of traveling the most: listening to his favorite music while driving his Alfa in the desert southwest, on a road intersecting a vast, unchanging panorama beneath an intensely blue sky ... where the possibilities seemed endless.

He stopped for gas in Lordsburg, just past the New Mexico border. He ate a submarine sandwich outside on a picnic table, watching the interstate traffic go by. Once again, he thought about the Medicine Wheel gift and the dream vision. Because of that, he resolved to go to Taos first. He couldn't ignore those things. He retrieved the Medicine Wheel from his luggage and tied it to the back of the rear-view mirror above the windshield: a fitting complement for the rest of his journey.

He reached into a box of cassettes and picked out Rachmaninoff's *Piano Concerto #3*. The first movements contained a familiar series of lyrical, evocative piano solos. The intensity of the music increased as he sped past Deming. A low, brooding undercurrent of strings evoked a sense of urgency in him. Other movements put him in a serene, almost euphoric, state of mind.

A road sign indicating the Las Cruces exit ahead shook him out of this strange, fluctuating mindset. He quickly merged into the far-right lane. The dangling Medicine Wheel rocked back and forth from the sudden lane change and caught his attention for a moment. The colors were in the appropriate alignment, according to what Sylvia told him, with white on top, black on the bottom, and the yellow and red on each side. Now he recalled another thing she mentioned about the Wheel; specifically, about how a person can't fully understand the meaning of life until they travel in all four directions –

Suddenly, he ditched the idea of going to Taos and gunned the Alfa past the exit.

After crossing the shadow of the overpass, he reasoned out the details of this burst of scrambled logic. No, he couldn't go north to Taos yet because he needed to travel the other three directions first. Otherwise, he'd fail at whatever he tried up there. Since he acquired the Wheel, he'd only driven south and east. No, he had to travel further east to New Orleans first, so he could drive *west* when he returned. Then he'd be on that all-important fourth direction from Las Cruces to Taos.

He raised his fist and shouted an emphatic "Yes!" This way, he could go to New Orleans, and when the time was right, go back to Taos and do some composing. A perfect solution.

The Rachmaninoff Concerto ended after he passed Las Cruces, so he turned off the radio to be alone with his thoughts without any distractions. Soon, he began to have doubts about the snap decision at the crossroads. The doubts continued to gnaw away at him as he drove past El Paso and toward the open country of west Texas. He couldn't help thinking about the moment he zoomed past the I-25 exit. All because of the sudden insight about the Medicine Wheel. But now he realized this was based only on Sylvia's version of it. Yet he used that tidbit of information as the ultimate factor to change course. The doubts eventually grew into genuine remorse. Briefly, he considered turning around and going back but ditched the idea.

He drove in a semi-trance on straight, flat stretches of the Interstate that seldom altered direction, and where the heat shimmered off the ground in some locations. Soon, he felt himself fighting off the same dread he had in South America – of being pursued by something. He roared past a semi-trailer truck, realizing he'd been going almost 100 mph. He slowed down and wondered how long he'd been driving so fast. The setting sun cast a faint orange glow on the distant hills and plateaus, with the terrain below in shadows. The bright residue of a jet contrail, the vapor slowly losing shape, stood out sharply above the hills in the darkening skies.

The creeping dread, coming back …

He snapped on the radio to a twangy country-rock station. Anything to chase the silence. The same frightful silence he always had during his childhood when he slept alone in the attic bedroom of that spooky old house, while the rest of the family slept in rooms on the main floor; how scared and angry he was, as if the family had abandoned him. And the many nights he huddled under the blankets to calm his fears while listening to music on his little transistor radio.

He searched for a different station and stopped when he picked up a raspy melody of a blaring saxophone solo – part of a song from a Gerry Rafferty album he owned titled "Get It Right Next Time." He fine-tuned the dial for a better signal. After it ended, he felt immensely relieved.

At dusk, he stopped in Fort Stockton for gas and food and decided to push on and crash at a motel in Ozona, about 100 miles away. About a half-hour past Fort Stockton, he almost drifted off the road. He pulled over at the next rest stop.

The predawn sky was ablaze with fiery hues of yellow and orange, merging into shades of indigo blue when he woke up. He unfolded the map to plot the route to New Orleans. He set it down, munched on an oatmeal bar, and thought about the shifting turn of events the day before. Once more, he convinced himself that going to New Orleans first was the right thing to do. Otherwise, the temptations there would always be on his mind. He didn't know how long he'd stay: perhaps a few weeks, a few months, a year, or more. Eventually, he'd head west

19

again and hopefully be able to contact Zena, thus fulfilling his destiny per the Medicine Wheel.

He merged back on I-10, shifted up to 5th and held the speed at eighty, listening to the sweet note from the engine. A few minutes past the rest stop, a burst of light exploded up from the horizon ahead, momentarily blinding him. He adjusted down the windshield visor as he drove through an endless landscape of parched dry earth and lifeless brush, into the rising sun.

3 x 5

We used these
ninja stars of
knowledge on weighty
test questions too
large to maneuver

(turn over)

on our own.

Caleb Bouchard

Forecast

A four a.m. fever fist
tightens in my throat –
a natural birth resulting
from several fingers of
bottom shelf bourbon and
five or more cross-eyed pints
(accuracy and precision are the
first things to punch out on Friday nights
or any night, really).
Suds and insomnia pinball
through the bloodstream,
spastic, double-exposed,
and here I am,
typecast as some pasty-haired
boozehound before the directorial morning light
has a chance to stride through the blinds
(the not-so-slant truth is that
I like it more than I dislike it).
Later today blood will blossom
in my tea mug, dust will
cling against the miniature disco ball
exiled in the corner of the front room,
flatlined church bells will drone at the top of the hour,
every hour, bluffing damnation,
sparrows will spy on sinners and saints alike,
unable to tell the difference.
Grizzled
arthritic clouds will stretch out their heavy arms
unbuckle their knees
and evaporate into eternity.
These are the things I can not control.

Caleb Bouchard

More for Tomorrow

Reading the latest *APR*, I pause to let the poems resonate –
a few today, more for tomorrow, same as the argument

a day ago that started with the a/c &
ended in bitterness: we put it down,

allowed our spite to spit up blood in silence.
Today we might talk about the gurgle in our throats,

while saving the juiciest remorse
for when our nerves have had their rest &

require sustenance. We placed leftover pizza
in the fridge. It won't be as good eaten cold;

worse reheated – it's there for us, lurking,
scenting the chill with pepperoni grease.

I sometimes tell myself one more poem,
one more slice. I'd waste the words &

make myself sick, bloated with bluster,
eating a hole through the world.

Ace Boggess

Dismissed

This therapist is a Gemini. Taken with her wit
after our first conversations, taken with the way
she cocks her head sarcastically when she barbs
me with a probing question, the way her funky
haircut does its own thing, I had a friend look up
our astrological compatibility in a book I didn't have.
Together, we are "Guardians of the Downtrodden."
I liked that. My last therapist called me "oppositional,"
said I acted like a child. In therapy, I search
for the resolve to save myself, but this attitude –
of Patti Smith in "Gloria," or Kurt Cobain in "Milk It"
numbs me out, renders me dumb. Anger peppers
my days. I adore and resent beauty. I am
"The Week of the Child;" my capacity for awe
is endless. I dare the world to raise a full orange moon
to a midnight blue sky. I dare the fawn to eat a leaf
from my fingers. I dare you to kiss me when I seem
least vulnerable. That's when I'm most likely to respond.
I will crush you like an ant. Or I won't, and we will
revel in the fact that we are alive. Right now.
It is the inescapability of moments, the trudging,
meandering, galloping along of them, that galvanizes so.
When we awake, there we are. There is no reason for it.
The reasons you invented deflate like an ego being dismissed
over the clink of cocktail glasses. We are all dismissed.

Amanda J. Bradley

Upon Reading Berryman's Sonnets

What so sexy in a sonnet lurks?
Is it between the lines as legs or sheets
hide wonders lovers clamber to repeat,
or is it the tradition that it works?
Does language force the mental tongue embark
on crevices and larks that tempt to heat
the flush and pulse of skin that suffers sweet,
such lush and ample games of toward remark?

If you, my dear, would love me half as well,
your touch incline me to such ecstasies
as when I read the pain in what you write,
I would not rise from bed to answer hell,
nor salvage purity on bended knees.
I dare you, love. Mindfuck me through the night.

Amanda J. Bradley

Philia

I paint my childhood best friend's nails
light green to match her eyes.
I try to be gentle with the cuticles and skin
picked and shredded from worry.

Her fingers get trapped in the knots in my hair
and the green paint smears through the black.

"We grow together," she says.
"I can't say that about anyone else."

In middle school, we'd compare photos.
Mark the changes from seventh to eighth grade.

"We are so
old," we said then, we say now.

I sip the pink moscato in my mug.
The proof of my impending adulthood.

She's wearing my high-school t-shirt to sleep.
And she starts to tear up when she sees me cry.

"Tell me something
you've never told anyone before."

McKenzie Bonar

It Is Me Or the SmartWatch

He knows your caloric intake –
you tell him when the smoothie
blends into a pink foam
dotted with sprinkles of kale –
before I know that you won't
be having any dinner. Not hungry.
I hear you ask him to play you
a song, and your earbuds mean
he has your attention, your devotion.
He has your cycles and REM
while I stare at him covering your skin,
as the moon covers sand,
pulsing with shushing waves,
as the lock over Fort Knox
covers the vault of dormant gold.

My sweet, though he measure your pulse,
he will never feel it.

So he can count your plodding steps;
does he feel the breeze of your
body in the hall? The look of you in heels?
He can forgive that eclair after dinner,
because you never told him, but
the chocolate smell lingers.
Behind his back, not mine, you
ate a pear that grew on our tree,
one he did not order through Clicklist.
With me you shared the grit and the soft interior.
He was not there for your
first ever glass of red,
or the sunset summer of 2008.
Love of my life, he holds you
like a branch holds an owl,
and he knows I am the
scurrying life you wait for.

Caleb Coy

Three Six-Year-Old Boys

There was something wrong with the boy next door. My mother
said he almost drowned
once and his brain
didn't get enough
oxygen. That's why
his arms flapped
when he walked
and he could only
grunt. His eyes were
all googly, too.
The other boy
lived in the dirty
green trailer. Trouble.
Did bad things
with firecrackers.
The girls
were afraid of him.
I was sent home from school. Bunchy Krill told Miss Kaplan
I smelled. Pointed
at me like I was
a country on that map
hung near the black board.
He grinned at me,
loved my humiliation,
made the class laugh.
Especially the girls.
Especially Jess.
I walked home stinking
and sticky with Accident.
The boy with googly eyes
and bad-boy turtle-killer
sat together on my stoop.
They knew I'd be
home early. After my
mother yelled, slapped and cleaned me up, I sat next to them.

Lenny DellaRocca

The Scoundrel's Last Refuge

A flag is an ugly thing, said my Uncle Max,
who knew ugliness when he saw it. A flag is for
pissing on, or burying, or burning. Whatever you do,
don't salute one. It will turn on you quick as
a mantis, taking your head and leaving your body
to sink in the mud. Pledge your allegiance rather
to the house finch who sings in the magnolia.
She will gladly serenade you without asking
which uniform you wear. This and more said
my uncle just before he died. We buried him
at night, illegally (a fact I'm sure he'd cherish),
in the shade of his big butternut tree, a refuge
in which he had found comfort during life.
Aunt Tilly sold the house to a rich and nasty neighbor
who, after chopping down the great butternut,
planted a flagpole. Poor Uncle Max. He really did
know ugliness when he saw it, and now he
decomposes beneath the thing he most despised.
Nobody needs my uncle to tell them that the flapping
of the neighbor's flag in the afternoon breeze
sounds nothing like the song of the house finch.
One day a red-winged blackbird perched on the metal
finial ball atop the flagpole. Well, this cinches it, thought
the blackbird, if humans truly prefer shiny steel to leaves
and flowers, then some among them must know that
they sing the world's doomsong. There are humans
who believe that birds share access to the spirits.
Just so, after a brief communion with my Uncle Max
(who lay beneath the concrete that anchors the pole
to the earth's crust), the blackbird rose up and, briefly
hovering there, dropped his bright viscous opinion
of the matter upon the boldly-colored cloth,
a kind of salute, before he flew off in the general
direction of the hills, which have yet to yield their
seventeen soft shades of green to the enemy, the enemy

who even now stands at attention, hand over heart,
a kind of prayer posture, a kind of silent admission
that the ribs form a cage around the very tenderness
that might once have been his greatest strength.

David Denny

Summer

My dad used to play the bar band circuit during most of my childhood
he and his friends would load up our trailer with their instruments
and I'd pile into the back of the van and we'd drive all the way into the city
for the weekend. Usually, the bartenders
would let me and my sister sit in the back of the bar to watch our dad
give us free Cokes and candy or bowls of popcorn to keep us occupied,
tell us how cool it was that our dad played music, that maybe
we'd grow up to be musicians ourselves someday, we'd be playing bars
just like this one someday. I never thought about being a musician myself
but I liked seeing my dad on stage, I thought that was super cool
and I could sing along with any Skynyrd or Neil Young or Beatles song
after hearing him and his band practice for hours and hours in the basement.

Sometimes he'd play street or county festivals,
and our mom would let us go out and explore
because she wanted to stay by the stage and watch our dad,
she wanted to dance to the music, and we weren't ever interested in that.
I'd spend hours watching grizzled bikers getting and giving tattoos
on a folding card table set up on the side of the road,
whole pigs gutted and roasted on spits and cut up to be passed out on paper
plates have drunk hippies call me over to give me lectures about life
recite random bits of poetry to me. But best of all, the musicians I knew on
stage would see me and shout out my name and ask me to get them a beer,
and I would run over to the keg, fill four or five plastic cups of beer
bring them over to the band, knowing everyone I knew from school could see me
even some of my teachers, who were probably writhing in disapproval
because I knew that here, in this place at least, I was pretty cool.

Holly Day

being

a frolick in the
woods naked at midnight
when two
sexy big-dicked freshly-turned-18-year-old boys
decide
to drink as much as they can
and spurt cum
as many times as they
can, they
keep count,
bottles, orgasms,
jizz galore
spotting the ground
musking the air
the future
just a fluffy dandelion seed
adrift on
the warm summer wind.

Carl Miller Daniels

Barefoot Summers

Farmer's daughter with toughened soles
from daily walks on sandy roads,
eyes cast down in concentration.
spying the delicate tracks
of sand aunts, their furry bodies of
black and orange, like tunnel tigers,
entrapping hapless prey.

Farmer's daughter with toughened soles
to wander pasture paths worn deep,
cattle passing to and from the barn
daylight and dusk,
lazy grazing through the day,
their red and white hides her definition
of what a cow should wear.

Farmer's daughter with toughened soles
in search of where her father works,
avoiding goat head stickers sharp enough
to penetrate her leathery feet
but worth the risk, to sit somewhere – a feed sack,
a tractor seat, a smooth wooden rail –
to learn the lessons of the soil.

Lyn Fenwick

Single Wide Trailer

He calls before midnight, slurring words but coherent.
It's a great setup he says, just gotta' wait a half hour,
she's getting rid of this schlub of a guy who showed up.
Who's she? Doesn't matter. She's like forty years old, slim,
got a sexy walk. Two kids in there but it isn't bothering
her. Come on. She's up for anything. I'm gettin' ready
to go to sleep. You crazy. This is a good thing man.
Nah. I'll pass. Come on. I don't wanna go back alone.
Why? I'm tellin' ya, you don't wanna miss this. I met
her in Barrett's bar. She lives in that trailer park
below the turnpike overpass. Crazy kinda broad,
wants any kind of fun. I'm gonna fuck her sure as shit.
You can fuck her too. At seventeen a crazy kinda grown
woman up for anything is a real draw, but frightening.
Whattya want me for? I'm pickin' up two six packs.
This is a sure thing. Gonna be wild. I mean wild bro.

The Broadway bus lands at Forty-Seventh St. He's there
with the beer, waiting in a doorway of a closed deli.
Two blocks over you go down a washed out road
with tossed cans and an old weather ruined sofa
discarded haphazardly. There's the single wide
seen better days tin can trailer. It looks dark inside.
You think the mook's gone? Fuck if I know. There's
nothin' goin' on in there, let's get out of here. He knocks
on the door. Knocks again. A tall thin dyed blonde
woman yanks the door open and laughs the way people
used to laughing in the face of misery sometimes do.
Baldy gone? your friend asks. Again the laugh, She steps
aside and we go in with our beer, nerves anticipating
God knows what. The children are a little more than that,
boy about seventeen, pudgy girl with nice lips and new
curves, probably fifteen, knees up with her arms around
them sitting in a chair by a formica topped little table.
The visitor chased away left a large cheese pizza.
Everyone eats, opening beers. The son goes out the door.

You look at the daughter. Your friend laughs
and the woman laughs and they go into the one
bedroom at the other end of the trailer. You down
a Budweiser, then another, courage in a bottle.
The boy returns, giggling. He seems demented in the way
future long term prison inmates are when young.
The daughter, whose name you think someone said was Melissa,
or Marla, tells the brother to go away but he won't. She tells
you to come on and you go behind the sheet separating
the bedroom from the rest of the small sad home. Your friend's
in bed with Mom. He tells you, come on, get in. The mother
laughs, says, leave him alone, she'll take care of him, won't you
baby. The girl's lip has formed into a pout. There are twin beds
in there. You lay down with her on the empty one. Your buddy
and the mom are fucking now and you feel frozen. The girl puts
a hand on your crotch. The son steps through the curtain,
a ball busting grin on his face. The mother shouts, get out of here
you perv. He giggles. She throws a pillow at him and he goes.
You kiss the daughter. The two of you strip down
        to your underwear.
She takes you in her mouth and you hear your friend say, lemme
get that thing over there and put it in you. The mother says,
anyone ever tell you you're crazy. The daughter stops, gets
off the bed with a blanket and lies on the floor. You wonder
what kind of life she's lived knowing it's just this kind of life
and probably will always be the same even after she's gone
from under the roof of her mother's sick world. When you hear
her quietly crying you get your pants and shirt back on,
wondering what the best way to get out of there might be.

Michael Flanagan

A More Perfect Union

I'm not asking for perfection.
(No nation is perfect.)
I'm not even insisting
America honors every promise enshrined by its Founding Fathers.
and yet …
we *can* do better.

A blueprint already exists.
to guide our way
to one nation indivisible,
Beer ad America:

A land of sky-blue waters and fun drunks –
where diverse yuppies play touch football
on Stinson Beach.

Beer ad America:
an America that doesn't see *everything* as blue or red,
nor *everyone* as black or white.
An America that only sees …
double.

Beer ad America:
where young, braless girls chill on couches
and listen to upbeat reggae music that assures
"Every little thing's going to be all right,"
Beer ad America:
Where lanky rap stars exchange greetings with sunbathers
while handing out free beer.

Beer ad America:
Forget *James* Madison.
who needs him?
We have Madison *Avenue*,
and it has shown us the way to a more perfect union.

A country not riven by class, religion and race,
but unified by Miller Time,
Spuds McKenzie,
and The Most Interesting Man in the World.

Let's all raise a glass to *that* America,
Beer Ad America:
One nation, slightly buzzed,
with Clydesdales and gusto for all.

One More Reason Not to Write Today

This morning,
as I browsed through the stacks
of the local bookstore,
I was comforted
to chance upon
several books on reincarnation
neatly displayed
on a shelf
labelled
"Time Management."

Eric Grow

Conversation in a Car

Sometimes on my monthly,
weekend visits after a long day
of taking city buses, walking
to all the places Jesse loves,
his mom picks us up before
dusk becomes pitch black.
While sliding into the back,
clicking his seat belt shut,
Jesse insists she turn the radio
on, tune it to his favorite station,
louder please. He asks endless
autistic questions regarding
a big bottle of Mom's ice-tea
for his refrigerator on Friday,
gondola rides and shopping
trips July 2025. Usually,
she'll ask about my flight,
where we ate, what I ordered.
i'll ask about Jesse's monthly
massages, last time he went
skiing, his new support staff.

Our conversation is polite,
targeted sentences filled
with purpose that sound
like a part time caregiver
speaking to a mom, distant
acquaintances touching base,
two people who never meant
anything to each other. Trying
to be funny, I'm tempted
to mention I'm getting old,
we better hurry, take that trip
to Paris she often talked about
not because I'm still feeling,
that kind of love or really want
to spend time with her, just

to change the tenor of my visits,
see if she still knows how
to laugh, rediscover things
that connected us, ways
we once talked to each other.

Maybe she won't hear me,
ask Jesse about our plans
for Saturday instead, dates
of my next visit. Her lips
could open in surprise,
shift into a smirk of dismissal,
an unexpected annoyance,
something to flick away
like a mosquito. Or maybe
her eyes would soften
like a butterfly's wing,
a hint of smile finding
it funny or remembering
any one of the many times
we were the best parts
of each other's lives.

Tony Gloeggler

Music

Once
I was like the winged guitar
Of Ritchie Valens
(A little bit of Texas rattlesnake)
That was in the age of the turntables
It was in the age of UNICEF,
Radio Free Europe, and the atomic bomb
And first a dove flew out of the guitar
It was flying towards Mexico over the cotton fields

Flew over the river that gleamed
With chemical wonder
And it was Mardi Gras down below
Where flambeaus were dancing in the streets
And the music must have been jazz
That caused the constellation to spin
On the point of a needle
After all, it was in the age of the guitar
It was in the age of the death of the romantic
And astronauts were busy proclaiming
The deconstruction of the moon

And then a dragon leapt out of the guitar
It rose as smoke over the Mississippi Delta
A dragon with a thirst so great
It cast a giant shadow on the world
And the needles fell into their grooves
They fell into the arms of those
Who rode a saxophone into the night
And there was Hendrix on the airwaves
All the way from Honduras
Jerry Lee Lewis hammering the ivory bones
And the dragon roared
Incinerating the cotton fields

And the radios took it all in
They sent messages to the fishing boats
That had strayed far out on the black water
And the universe hummed in the strings
It said we might be nothing but notes
In the mind of God
And the planets were dancing to celestial music
Angels of crystal were flying over the roof
Strangers were knocking at the door
Begging shelter
The night was green with the beginning of love.

Jay Griswold

Jim Morrison

Jim Morrison, you are a runaway train,
An angel of stone who stands guard
Over the black tolling of bells,
You are the bull on his knees in a circle of blood,
The bottomless note no one hears,
The cry that comes from the other side of God.
You are a field sown with dead crows.
It's impossible to talk to you.
You are the black cape that Lorca wore
When he soared over the rooftops of Grenada.

Yes. And you are also the final assault
Of butterflies, a lullaby for children
Who have fallen asleep in the snow.
You are a lost letter blown for a thousand miles,
And the last poem found in the pocket
    Of Attila Jozsef.
Attila Joseph, the engineer muses.
Yes, I remember him,
But I never ran him down with my train.
He was always trying to burn down Budapest
All by himself, the crazy bastard.

Jay Griswold

Christmas

It's Christmas Eve
And I'm wondering why I'm still alive
There were so many women who wanted to kill me
There were so many bombs that didn't explode
Sometimes I could kiss my own loneliness
These days when I feel too lonely
I go down to the local mall
And mingle with the wandering herd
Who are all gazing intently into their smart phones
(I'm sure in the future human beings
Will be born with a smart phone
Instead of a left hand)
They glance up occasionally to see where they are
They are all searching for something that will make them happy

I too wander
Down hallways ablaze with lights
Where music flows like a chorus of angels
And because I want to get into the spirit of things
I search the crowd
For some revelation about the species
Or only a smile on a pretty face
I walk through the valley of my own shadow
And feel my loneliness slip away
As if I traveled under a starry sky
On the road to Bethlehem
And the cradle of that most famous dead man of all
         Jesus Christ.

Jay Griswold

Washington Street

I'd thrown a handful of rocks at a car
passing by my grandmother's house
on the suggestion of Walter
who lived down the street. I wasn't sorry.

Only surprised the car had stopped,
that the person inside was a person at all,
then angry she'd marched to the door
of my grandmother's house, told. I frowned

at that car and its driver, the boy who slipped away,
my own failure to hide in the ditch
and my parents' divorce the month before.
How brief the catharsis, pebbles pinging

against metal and glass, power and anger
jettisoning gravel and sand.

Lisa M. Hase-Jackson

Padfoot the Grim

Susan swallowed vodka.
Prayed for dreamless sleep.
Eyelids drifted closed.
Limp hand dropped the bottle.
Mouth opened in a snore.

Padfoot the Grim wriggled
through a crack in the window.
Red eyes gleamed.
Slavering jaws opened
in a rictus grin.

The black hellhound
of death and depression
waved his skeletal tail.
Conjured explosions
and screams.

Susan's best friend
whose face was shredded
by shrapnel.

The lieutenant
who whimpered
the name of his child
as he died.

The enemy soldier
who held Susan's hand
as he bled out.

Susan's own right leg
devoured by an IED.
Phantom pain
never died.

Alicia Hilton

Dip me in honey and throw me to the lesbians

(After Diane Seuss)

Gorged myself on her Bacardi Breezers, when it was cool
to skull red rum, first year uni, opened in some student's
loungeroom, momentary megalith, eskies to rival David's
Goliath. It was cheaper that way, get legless then foray,
Dingos, she called the club, like the canine, only bereft it
was, of dogs, nevertheless, full of bitches, witches, she called
the competition, no cauldrons or broomsticks, plenty of warts,
though, I wouldn't know. I didn't care what I drank, the picture
I portrayed, bevvied my body weight in gin, Wednesdays
through Saturdays, made actuality go away. She had no idea
what I'd done, until I righted myself and she bummed, us a ride
across the bridge, north to south, earlier, in a room with a guy,
wedged like a case of Chlamydia, she was, only guessing, still,
I'd heard rumours, girls like us, broke into detachable parts,
none of them equal, one part, always spilling, put in appearances
Mondays, Tuesdays, the other parts starving, terrorised boys,
Fridays, Saturdays, T-shirts they made in our honour. Dickheads,
like starlets we were, doms unto ourselves. *Dip me in honey*,
bubble ink in pussy pink they read, *and throw me to the lesbians*.

Kylie A Hough

Jesus Freak

I'd consider dating Jesus, if he flew down from heaven, or
wherever he fucked off to, to get away from humanity, or my
brother, if he wasn't my brother, or married, well, okay, even if
he was married, until last week, when I decided I'm not sure
what my worth is, but that it sure as shit equates to more than the
second coming someone else's husband never offered, me, a
bona fide Jesus Freak, no idea what the bible says, no memory of
attending Sunday School, no favourite story of Jesus I can
recount at Christmas time, unless you count the one where he
turns water into wine, I loved that one, not so much, now,
though, I don't drink, not since I dreamed about my ex losing a
battle with arsenic, blasphemous, I know, years after Jesus
rocked up, mid therapy, mid spew, my guts, my psychologist, it
was sudden, my eyes went first, rolled back in my skull, ecstasy,
off my head, in a clinical setting, too, there's always a first time,
I mean, I saw him, clear as crystal meth, and if Jesus makes an
appearance, you know you're good, for something more than
nights alone, crying yourself to sleep, lonelier than a leper in a
colony of Victoria's Secret models, which brings me back to
Jesus, why I'd probably date him, maybe even fool around, he
had a soft spot for Mary, the bad one, some stories even say,
he loved her.

Kylie A Hough

m(O)ther

(For Diane Seuss)

To be frank, you're not my mother because you won the Pulitzer,
who is that anyway, listening, seeing, I mean it helps, but it's not
the be all and end all, more like the rainbow after rain, except
when it's muggy, fuck that, and hail in November, too,
the break that mends with a riddle, half-rhyme, perfect time,
the gravity of fragmentation, your possibilities are Piscean, your art
shows me mine, on occasion, the egg falls off the wall, but the essence
is the point, humpty, the shell, the yolk, how about it, does it matter,
for instance, hydro glyphs in the ice or something or other, smirking
faces, cymatics, litany of light, then salt, you are oceans, glorious
Other, not awards, nor ceremony, not fellowships nor grants,
not the way you don't puke when I rush, gush, no, you're oxygen
powered, whore witted, probably stretch-marked, like me, the real
deal, a witch in drag, transmorphic, otherwise known as, hydrogen.

Kylie A Hough

I Never Knew Bukowski, and Most of Our
Mutual Friends are Dead

There's a shot of bourbon waiting for me at the Reno Room in
Long Beach, California. Not my favorite bar, not the seedy dive
it appears in Buk's poems. But the one where all the young poets
went to chase his ghost,

like he were shuffling back there, between the pool tables and
the upscale Mexican food. Even Long Beach changes; even
Worcester changes; even all these working class towns I felt so
comfortable in transmute to something new over time. That, or
face extinction.

In Worcester, there's a tapas bar where Emma Goldman's ice
cream shop once stood. The restaurant actually *is* one of my
favorites, although the prices make me plot sedition. I don't
think about anarchy when I'm eating there, at least not often.
There's not likely many alive who remember Emma Goldman
personally. She died eighty years ago. Bukowski died in 1994. I
knew lots of people who knew him.

A lot of those folks are gone now – lost to cancer or COVID; or
moved to Vegas, which is practically the same. People only get
to transform so many times before we expire, before we vanish
into the stories of those we leave behind, and when they're gone,
if we're lucky, our work remains.

Buk's poems don't care that I was hit or miss with them. They'll
live on regardless. I liked FrancEyE's poems better, and I worry
her writing will vanish with each tide. I liked Gerry Locklin's
poems, too, but he planted so many they'll be turning up for
decades. Some days, I don't like anything I've written, but that
makes no difference as to whether any of those words survive or
not. That one's not up to me.

Will the young poets ever turn up at Nick's in Worcester looking
for my ghost? Will they buy a Manhattan because they know

that's what I drank there? Will it change by then, quirky cabaret
bar transformed by proximity to a baseball stadium?

Who knows? Nothing to do with me.

By the time that all happens
I'll be somewhere else.
Maybe haunting a bar
that was never my favorite,
drinking whiskey
in another time, another place
when everything was filled with starlight.

Victor D. Infante

Deadhead Sticker on a Cadillac

The TV commercial makes the implicit promise that when I take
that cruise line there will be liquor and drugs, and a sex a
machine, and that we'll dance like hypnotized chickens. I
suspect they're overselling it.

You can plaster songs on commercials like beige paint, but it
doesn't change what those songs mean, or what they meant when
we were young and slamming our bodies hard in the pit

of a dingy club, where the Damned were electrifying on stage
and the lower-case damned were tying off their arms in
bathroom stalls, shooting up junk, and all I can think is, "You
paid for the ticket, you should at least dance."

I was 16 when a Goth girl kissed me amid the cacophony of a
midnight screening of *The Rocky Horror Picture Show*. It was
after "Time Warp" and "Sweet Transvestite," but years before I
understood some girls only kissed to be kissed, that it was no
promise of anything.

An Airbnb commercial plays "Time Warp" over images of
happy families and sometimes I see it and think of that kiss, an
ephemeral, anonymous moment – lust and experimentation, in a
dangerous place where we felt safe breaking our hearts …

… or maybe the reverse. Maybe those midnight showings were a
safe space to be a little dangerous. Is that the feeling America is
trying to sell back to me now, as Iggy Pop, the Damned, the
Clash and *Rocky Horror Picture Show*

become the nostalgia of jingle, like The Who did before them, or
the Stones, or every work of art that once spoke to our need to
feel alive in a world that seemed too ordered by far, too sterile,
too safe?

I didn't much care for the Eagles back then, but that song by Don Henley still stuck with me: *Out on the road today / I saw a Deadhead sticker on a Cadillac ...*

I think of that song a lot more often, these days ... *don't look back*, sings Don. *You can never look back.* It's true. Look back at the past too long and you'll take away all the wrong lessons:

what you learned from the dancing and the kisses and the drugs, from the vanished lovers and buried friends, from the thousand mistakes forged into nostalgia, into a piece of your soul that someone else is trying to sell.

Victor Infante

Only One Way

Stand back.
I'm a loser

who eats her heart in hell.
I'm HIV to you,
death in blood.

There's only one way,
stand back.
I'm a loser

don't tell me:
you need me.
I'm the echo
that pretends
to reply intelligently.

Stand back,
I'm the loser

so don't tell me
you love me.

Enjoy my silence.
My sentence.

My name is this broken machine
that forever
and forever
has neither voice nor void,
only pieces
Of what could have been

Akiva Israel

O N E

Don't look for my body.
   Act as if there's none.
Don't
   act as if there were, apart from this
  body of text, body with male sex, race …
   I'm not my body. Has my penis soul?
  Body: carnal curriculum of touch
    I'm sure is useless: meat spoiled in the sun:
   my beige-breast earth: sloppy swamp of nerve
    mashed in time's enzyme-thick, acid-pink pouch.
   I: one-penny morsel
    smashed in death's huge mouth of midnight moonlight.
      United with a body, I'm nobody;
      dis-united, mere fact there's this poem: I'm somebody.

Akiva Israel

Secret Memorial for a Dead Prince

I shut all the doors.
    Why do you think that might be?
My room – moonless in the dark – I undress there, aware:
     the moon's full
    I: alone animal atop a used bed.
Still in bed, I picture my prince
    in life, in my head; nude – I, inside him,
still … rub what still works, thrust my man-museum.
    Sin? How!? Self-sex to my love's mental picture
honors his memory more than a tomb
    birdshit on tombs
turd-embalmed tomb,
    by stone toddler-angelic eyes shit-faced.

        Done, secret goodbye: it's not a small thing
        Son, and like that solitary pleasure – it's short.

Akiva Israel

Lori Jakiela

Out Here in the Open with the
Sunlight and the Trees

I point my camera at the man with a camera.

"It's a goddamn postcard day," my editor said, and rubbed his stomach like he'd swallowed the day down.

The park, the zoo, the leaves beginning to turn.

I always want to take my time, to find something beautiful and surprising, but my editor believes in efficiency.

"Just shoot the bear," he said as I was leaving. "People love that fat ass."

Gus the Polar Bear, New York City's star attraction, more photographed than any celebrity. Gus had his own paparazzi. Every season, Gus would show up on the news, as regular as the weather and traffic reports.

My editor knows Gus sells. Pictures of Gus make the terror of the day's headlines more digestible, maybe.

What my editor doesn't know – today there will be an accident. It will be horrible, a baby, and I will be there to see it.

"Heard," I said, but I knew that for me, on a day like this, Gus would be an afterthought.

***

At the park, I took pictures of an old man selling *coco helado* on a corner. The red antique cooler, the man's wide silver blade, his change-purse hands as he dusted the ice block with sugar then shaved it like a callous. When the police came by, the man hid the blade and held still, like he couldn't be seen if he didn't move, like he was impenetrable, behind glass.

The police kept going. The man lifted his blade again, his magic trick, and went on shaving.

Pretty soon it will be too cold to sell shaved ice. I wonder what the man does in the off-season, if he makes enough to get by.

When my editor hired me a year ago, he said, "You won't get rich, but you will die trying." I'm sure he's used that cliché many times, but he laughed loud, snorted even, as if he thought it up on the spot special for me.

Before this, I gigged – bartender, line cook, engagement and new-pet shoots. I liked bartending best. You can tell a lot about a person from their drink order – extra dirty martini; fuzzy navel; whiskey straight, two fingers; whatever's on draft. I love the way people in bars tell secrets. I love strangers I can imagine as friends, the easy intimacy of that.

Taking pictures is a funny thing, intimate too, but one-sided because the people you're shooting often don't know you're shooting them.

"Look natural," I say when they do know. A ridiculous thing to say.

There's a lot of waiting – for the light, for the right angle. It gives a person time to imagine, to think.

"Put the camera down," my daughter started saying as she got older and tired of posing. "Just be a person. Just be here."

But I couldn't. I always felt it – everything temporary, so easy to lose.

"I want to remember," I'd told my daughter, but sometimes even with pictures, I forget. My daughter's first steps. When her hair turned from blonde to brown. When she was so small, a loaf of bread really, so light I could carry her in a sling across my chest. When she stopped telling me her secrets.

"Vault that," she'd said, and I turned the invisible lock on my lips. I tossed the key I'd made from air over my left shoulder. Always my left.

"For luck," I said, though I don't know when I began to think like that.

***

The old man with the *coco helado* – his name is Juan Carlos. He's 68, lives alone in Kew Gardens. I take photos but I have to follow up with details – name, age, neighborhood. I try to catch people's voices, too, just a line maybe, something uniquely theirs.

Years ago, I did another gig – this time at the obituary desk of a small-town newspaper. I was a kid, not even 20, and once I made a mistake and spelled a name wrong. The dead man's family called to complain, and the publisher called me into her office.

The publisher's office smelled like rubbing alcohol and newsprint and the menthol cigarettes she smoked on the sly and dropped out her window. On the ground outside her office, there was a mound of red lipstick-splotched butts, a cigarette graveyard.

"The only time most people get their name in the paper is when they die," she said. "You cannot fuck that up. What the hell's wrong with you?"

It's impossible to run a graceful correction of someone's obituary. For years now, I've compensated by making sure I get the names and words right for every photo I shoot.

"Don't fuss. Just get some of that 'Humans of New York' happy crap," my editor says about what he wants in a caption of a photo that is not a photo of Gus the polar bear.

Juan Carlos wanted people to know his *coco helado* is the best in the city. He wanted people to know he makes enough to afford his own place.

"You write that," he said, poking at my notebook. "Lives alone. My own place."

He gave me a free *coco helado*. "If you close your eyes, you think it's real coconut, like on an island," he said.

He said, "Maybe you come away with me."

He said, "Your lucky day!"

He said, "How old are you?"

I wanted to say *too old and too young for you,* but Juan Carlos was charming, and I didn't want to ruin things.

"My daughter would miss me," I said, and Juan Carlos said, "She can come, too, if she's beautiful like you."

My daughter is 30 now. She is, I'm sure, so beautiful. She lives in LA.

"Time zones," my daughter says about why she doesn't call.

***

It's getting late and I know my editor will be getting twitchy.

"Let's put the dead in deadline, people," he'll say and snort-laugh.

Off to my left, the man with the camera looks through his lens. Of course he's shooting Gus.

"Just shoot the goddamn bear and be done with it," my editor would say.

Instead, I take a series of shots of the man with the camera, both our shutters clicking, all those tiny locks, secrets vaulted and carried still.

I carried my daughter with me as long as I could – that front sling, then a backpack. I wanted her close. I wanted her safe. I wanted her with me always, for her, for me, for my loneliness.

"Smother," she said, laughing. "Get it? S-mother."

What were some of those secrets she told me? I vaulted them so deep maybe they're lost.

"That was a long time ago," my daughter says now.

Later, about the pictures of the man with the camera, my editor will say, "Well this is very fucking postmodern," and I won't know if he likes them or not.

Probably not.

***

Gus the polar bear is famous because he can't stop swimming. Gus the polar bear's glass tank is so clear it's invisible. I can shoot head-on and

59

not get a glare. I can shoot like there's no barrier between us. The water is popsicle blue. The ice caps are mounds of *coco helado*. Behind Gus, a movie screen – films of polar bears in Alaska to trick him into thinking he's not alone.

"Neuroses bred by loneliness," the animal psychologist who's assigned to Gus says.

Gus swims relentlessly across his enclosure because of stress – *classic anxiety*, the psychologist says. The psychologist's salary is paid by a donor, rich, anonymous, an animal lover, probably neurotic, probably lonely.

This is New York City, Central Park, the epicenter of the rich and neurotic, the anonymous and lonely. In Alaska, where Gus is from, road crews set up perimeters of spotlights and sharpshooters to keep polar bears from eating workers on the night shifts. Sometimes that works. Sometimes not.

"Another of your fun facts," my daughter would say, and roll her lovely eyes.

I like my job. Most days, it's all I have, and I want to keep it, so I shoot the required pictures of Gus. I get close-ups of his massive paws, claws the size of meat hooks that gouge and scrape the ice the city manufactures for him. I shoot the movie screen bears. I get close-ups of Gus's long snout, his panicked eyes. I think of the polar bears in old Coke commercials, cuddly bears in knit scarves and hats, kicking back with ice-cold sodas.

Some years ago, Coke dropped the bears – polar bears being a threatened species, polar ice caps melting, not a good look, Coca-Cola corporate said – and went back to Santa instead.

"Did you know Santa was invented to sell Coke?" I'd told my daughter when she was young. "All that red and white."

"Fun facts," my daughter said and sighed.

What kind of mother tells her daughter about Santa like that? I should call and apologize. I should say something like, "I wanted to shield you from the world," or some other empty impossible thing.

***

Across the way, another man with another camera is taking pictures of a beautiful woman with a tangle of auburn curls. She holds a baby. She pulls the baby close. They touch noses. She looks like her, and she looks like her. I love catching stuff like this. They could stay like this forever, out here in the open with the sunlight and the trees.

The light is perfect. The shadows, perfect. I zoom in on this bit of beauty and shoot and shoot. I remind myself to get the woman's name later, the name of the baby, where they live, what they love most about New York City in the fall.

"Ah autumn in New York," my editor says about pretty shots like this one. "Makes you forget the smell of piss and garbage."

The baby is happy. She reminds me of when my daughter was little. I should call my daughter, tell her about Juan Carlos and this day with the sunlight pouring down through a sieve of leaves and branches.

"A sieve," I'll say, though she hates when I talk in pictures, and besides I'm on deadline, and she's busy, always busy.

I adjust the aperture to let in more light. The woman's hair is the color of red maple. The baby lets go of her mother's hair and spreads her little arms wide.

"Smile," the man with the camera says and I shoot him as he frames everything he loves and holds like a present.

My daughter's first word was Spanish, *abre,* open. When she said it, she spread her arms. When she said it, she waved. Hello. Goodbye.

This baby is so happy, alert and smiling.

Somewhere behind us Gus swims back and forth in his safe blue terrible world.

"A lunatic, like everyone else in this city," my editor said, and propellered his arms to make like he was swimming.

The Alaskan bears in the movie wag their heads.

61

Somewhere Juan Carlos sharpens his blade on a leather strap.

The man and I frame our shots just as a branch starts to fall, forty feet up. The branch is heavy, I can tell, later, in the photo, though I don't hear the crack.

"Put the camera down," my daughter would say, but I keep shooting. "Please."

The sunlight pours down. The woman smiles. The baby looks up, reaches, *abre,* open.

"The baby didn't even cry," a bystander will say. "That's how I knew it was bad. She didn't make a sound."

The Miracle of Forgetting

The good days are his Marlon Brando Godfather days
and old cop shows, eating cashews, and telling stories
about sticking it to the foreman while he worked the line.
Doling out insults disguised as jokes and remembering
nights in Brooklyn, cold but the ocean still calling him
to walk along the boardwalk, salt stuck on his skin.
And when I try to make conversation, him yelling,
"Shhh, you're going to make me miss this part."

I don't know the exact moment of his transition,
when my dad forgot so much of who he was
that he forgot he had a tough time being kind.

He offered me a hundred thousand dollars
with so much sincerity I didn't have the heart to tell him
he doesn't have that kind of money. Those are his bad days.
When he surprises me with a scarf I don't need from some
random internet website and tells me how much he loves me.
Tells me how grateful he is for things I've done for him.
Asks me if I want the last can of cream soda he has in his
refrigerator because it's his favorite. And he saved it for me.

"Let's go back to San Francisco. Pier 39. Me, you,
and your sister had such a good time when we went
that summer. You two, always with the secrets
and chit-chatting." Only, he hadn't come.
She and I wanted to walk the Embarcadero alone.
But I didn't tell him that. And I didn't tell him why.

Sarah Mackey Kirby

All Those Ghosts Playing Harmonica on Bourbon Street

They run through fingers of wild haired twenty-something
lost boys. Strumming three-peat Bob Dylan on Jackson Square
ledges, guitar cases open for dollar bills. Those ghosts.
The ghosts of all their pasts. With them still.
The scared kind, the wandering kind,
plucking back-home beatdown heartache
a riff at a time. They eat cheap fast food on concrete
between songs. Real live ghosts tasting mustard
and pickle remnants through lips that wished
they were tasting star drop air, tasting hope,
tasting girls so beautiful their tongues shine
like treasures in the moonlight.

They play harmonica. "Baby Please Don't Go"
Muddy Waters attitude. Haunting their hopes at
New Orleans open-mic-night bars on Bourbon Street
with the bluesiest soul stripped down to skeleton.
Still escaping creaky front porch swings and wind chimes.
Echoes of home. Sad walls. Those ghosts. Now downing
cold beer. Wishing it was some expensive vintage
Sazerac that would make people take notice; give
them the lucky break they can't ever seem to find.

Those nighttime ghosts that spray paint hell through
tired arms and smell of creole breath and Almond
Verbena flowers. The ghosts hide out in the city.
Outside buildings. Inside bodies. In cussing mouths
and crying eyes and street dancer legs, popping and floating
and spinning and moonwalking on bead-strewn avenues
to take up the time 'til something better comes along.
Some river's current that pulls them toward possibilities.
Where memories crawl into mausoleums
and jazz lights up the sky.

Sarah Mackey Kirby

Boardwalk Bijou

The morning bicyclers were not out yet
and dunes hid me, hungover, half asleep.
I knew she could not see me watching them
as they came to the boardwalk hand in hand,
a grandmother with a child about four.

Her gray hair blended with the gray of dawn,
and took a hot rose frost from the red tinge
of first light bouncing off the purple clouds.
She sat the child formally on the bench,
as though ushered into a theatre,
folding her hands in delicate white gloves,
her pocketbook carefully in her lap.

The new sun free above the horizon –
the bench now small against the grandeur of
a bonfire sky on molten metal waves –
a tear reflects like mirror on her cheek,
I made the trip so you wouldn't miss this,
the girl yawns early blue eyes at our show.
I warm to an all-encompassing gold
and the maternal heat of a new day.

Craig Kirchner

Dejeuner

Sparrows gathered on the veranda,
we eavesdropped on nearby lovers,
hand fed one another tapas,
swigged lewd licks on Czech beer.

Under the table you hiked your skirt,
opened your thighs around my knee,
animated codes with delicate hands,
laughed about our first time.

Surrounded by leg, birds, crumbs,
and curious voyeurs
wanting to share your smile,
hungry to stay young, touched,
needing a subtle strangeness
with an afternoon break.

Craig Kirchner

Zack Kopp

There Ain't Nowhere But Here

THIS time last week there was this broken-down dog head stuck over there, and everyone and his mother kept coming around here trying to pry it loose, getting wild tearing up the pavement and everything. Some dirty kids came out of the old gas station to throw rocks at it and look at it. Clouds of flies started swarming around it. No one had ever heard of such a thing or wanted to carry it around with them, so no one would put it away, whatever had first entranced them. The broken-down dog head kept lying there, seemed like no one would ever put it away. Lying there in the street, just being ignored and denied by all the citizens out of fear or disgust or the refusal to admit its existence. What would it do to our morals?

Three kids were drinking some watered-down piss under a black tarpaulin outside a gas station. The watered-down piss was supposed to be vodka, but the makers would just use whatever they could get fermented fast for a nickel and call it whatever they figured most people was out looking for. One kid called Rat-Eyes was always complaining about that poor quality piss, that's what they called it, but the others tried cheering him up. "This stuff comes from the factory!" "This is the best in three counties!" The other two kids, Carlos and Sweet Tooth, loved drinking that gasoline piss as much as Rat-Eyes, but they wanted to figure out how to resell the stuff out the back door if they could, and Carlos was always working out a complicated plan of how they were going to do this, but it never happened. "Just give the word," assured Sweet Tooth, spitting out a stream of clear matter. "I'll be ready." There was a blackjack concealed in his backpack, unnoticed by some. Others saw it in there and wondered, "What the hell's he planning?" Or they figured he was just showing off. A lot of people saw it in there. They all wrote gossip about having been there when it happened in their hot yearbooks later that month. Otherwise it was just a black backpack. Heavy metal stickers on it. Accepted by no one. Looking out of his window down the street, Sam could tell it was three different people because they had different hairstyles. Otherwise the kids looked almost exactly alike, scrawny, pinched-in features like all the houses around here.

It was a sunny city. Two winos walked around outside during lunch-break hour while Sam watched, imagining what they were talking about. Up and down the outdoor mall they walked, glowing with that special sunny pride a wino feels when he's got a good knife in his pocket. They were winos with knives in the city. One had a pocketknife with traditional folding blade. The other one had a Buck knife in his boot, made by a traditional Western knife-maker of old, last name of Buck. One of the winos had once known a guy named Sam Buck claimed to be the descendant of that same genius and probably was or maybe not. That's how things went in the city. Got scrambled and crazy. One's name was Alabama. He admitted his own limitations. He was obsessed with it. "I'll walk over there, a distance of twenty or twenty-five feet, and my legs will have no trouble carrying my 195 pounds. that distance. No way!" Then he'd look around, satisfied. "No way!" his imaginary audience cheered in agreement. "But just ask me to walk three HUNDRED and fifty FEET, carrying a weight of 30 pounds …" and he shook his head sadly. "There's just no way," the crowd in his head agreed. Meanwhile, the other hobo's hands were continually jumping trains or clambering over lumps of coal or getting flat out on rotgut in some alley or plunging into a hard-earned bath with a wrinkled newspaper after another hot day of grubbing around in the grime. Sam noticed through his binoculars that sometimes the left hand would be scuttling over an imaginary fence or around the side of an old shack. Meanwhile his right hand would be coming along like a train, and at just the proper moment in the hobo's conversation, the left hand would take flight, as if jumping off some craggy rocks, then landing smack on the right one, as if jumping right into a train, at the exact proper conversational time for him to say that in sign language. He had it all worked out like a rhythm. Other times his left hand would start digging around in his back pocket as if trying to burrow out some secret entrance. All he wanted was 99¢ but time kept on hurtling forward without him.

Down the street from those winos and right around the corner from Rat-Eyes and them, Sam had moved into another faceless suburban nightmare apocalypse neighborhood and he started digging a hole in the backyard. Every day after work at the corporate assembly line he would come home in his truck and go out back and just start digging. He didn't know why. Deeper and deeper he dug each afternoon from 4 to 7. The complex he lived in was surrounded by hills. All night you heard him screeching way off in the hills over all the worms he thought he'd killed without looking. Was he trying to unearth hidden cables, to learn what eldritch currents fueled this cookie cutter suburban nightmare apocalypse above, or trying to tunnel his way out of the endless repetition? He wasn't sure, but as long as he kept on digging that hole in his backyard, there would always be a way out of his other everyday concerns. One day the first inhabitants were gonna return. He didn't wanna be caught blinking when that happened. One day after work he was down there digging and discovered what resembled an unrecognizable corpse. They have buried dead bodies down here, he realized, and Hey, I can bury dead bodies down here, and maybe they will come back to life, like in the ancient Russian tradition! Working on it had strange hallucinatory effects he might never get to the bottom of. Sometimes when he was down there digging, working on the hole, all time would stop. It was like he could see all the people standing there, frozen, drinks in their hands, and he would go around the room putting pinches of the strange powders he'd been given into their drinks before snapping his gloved fingers and watching everything go back to normal again, people circulating, engaged in casual conversations with each other, laughing, never knowing what they'd been given. And what WERE these strange powders? My God, what was this strange imaginary party world in his mind? Who were all these people, projected symbols of his own life, or mysterious unsuspected psychic counterparts of Us All? Well, it hardly matters, he decided. I am just a dumb guy down here digging this hole in my backyard to get out of here or break into somewhere else. He decided the imaginary party in his mind with all the powders and the drinks he'd envisioned was probably some kind of weird lesson designed specially for his mind to teach him the meaning of systematic nonattendance, and paradoxic simultaneous attainment of – well, shit – he would never understand the specifics of it that way! Sam climbed up out of the hole in his own backyard and wiped his hands on his grubby jeans, looking around. An old man was sitting in his car on the street. He looked motionless there, sitting still as if frozen in time for a second. Then he started the engine and the little car drove off. A little dog went running down the street after it. Everything got smaller and smaller then went back to normal. A trick of the light? Perhaps.

That sinister backpack was an idea abandoned by everyone a long time ago. At the time the news broke, no one even suspected what had been inside besides a simple threatening-looking blackjack. Thirty pounds of powder explosives, that's what. I don't know what kind, I'm no bomb expert, but I hear nitroglycerine was involved, but if that was true, they would never have made it all the way to the cafeteria before exploding, so maybe that was just some scare they talk about like anthrax powder, which has not been added to any explosive mixtures yet, that I know of. But people are always looking for new, more horrible ways to disfigure and harm each other's bodies, and someone has probably tried it by now. Meanwhile the spirits keep having fun just a few inches away all the time. So who blew up the three rat kids? Sam wondered. Did they do it to themselves? We all participated in the rotting of civilization, all unknowing of the party that was always going on in this stupid neighborhood of money and deals and bad feelings.

The spirits were only trying to give mankind a good name after all the misdeeds piling up. They were doing it to honor themselves, dead or not. If the spirits had stayed in that backpack, the roof never would have been blown off this shaky dirty town. And then what? No more devilish deals for the tricksters, no more happy candy for the frivolous. And what good is a world like that? So people left the backpack lying there, ignoring every incidental noise. A bunch of us went out to the ball field a few minutes before it blew up. Later we were suspected of being in on it, or else why would we distance ourselves for no reason like that, and they questioned us, but I don't think anyone knew anything in the game of facts it became soon after. All these reporters kept trying to capture the evaporated facts from that lost afternoon. But that was a long time ago.

Despite Sam's abnormal need for strangeness and an all-consuming desire to be alone unless romantically entangled or busy getting something done requiring the help of others, community seemed to be the cure for his strange blindness, developed after all those days and nights of digging deeper into the hole in his backyard, continually dropping to new levels of flattened clay, proving this was either a project lasting for centuries, or something had been buried way down here before. Why question his logic? A madman! Seeing parties in his mind! He wanted to appear on a game show. Yes, that will be the perfect place for a madman like me, he reflected. Yes, he would joke with the game-show-host, smiling at the other guests. Or maybe he should be a game show host! His whole culture was perfectly designed for it. They had been training everyone since grade school. Yes, there are always two sides to a community like this one, Sam pondered, staring into the void for a moment. But there was no more time for speculation! Not now! He had to keep digging. After a few more spadefuls, the blade started tilting to the side and he had to climb out and go rummaging for a screwdriver, then he came back down using a rope ladder and continued heaving the backbreaking spadefuls of heavy brown clay up onto the surface somehow using brawn and brute strength engendered by all that feverish mad digging. That's when he first noticed the binoculars on sale at the hardware store.

Rat-Eyes was the final survivor. He crawled away from the blast with one mangled claw hand, removing any fingerprints. This last part is little-known but the eldritch claw-hand was later replaced by a prosthesis, and he became a high school chemistry teacher. All those little equations reminded Rat-Eyes of the deadly powders mixed in his youth to blow things up, but he fought to suppress it. Because of this he was an unusually harsh disciplinarian with his students, rapping their knuckles with a long wooden ruler, and sometimes behind the ears, too.

Often they were really misbehaving but sometimes Rat-Eyes would claim to have averted something that had been about to happen, removing all possibility of a proper defense. This was all due to his own mangled tortured youth of blowing things up for no reason, or reasons he made up himself. One more sad little life driving along down the street in a little Volkswagen. Right after the blast, Rat-Eyes had escaped into a nearby store that sold mannequins looking for help but there was no one but fake people there. He ran out. Was he looking for the truth or was that just a coincidence? Rat-Eyes was never associated with any misdeeds and later went on to his own small suburban glories and institutional abuses like everyone else. Even kids who had been sitting in the bleachers more than thirty feet away, now dead before their time, represented by chalk outlines, all because of what he did. It was all part of life's happy mixture.

The two winos kept walking around with their knives, they didn't know any better than anyone else all the forces that drove them, or where they were headed. They just kept going, bent on getting another good drink of rotgut. One of their victims that night turned out to be a marriage counselor. They read that in the newspaper. The winos took her string of pearls and all the money in her purse and left her bleeding in an alley like a stuck pig, later laughing together about how ironic it was, considering how they were all three married together in some strange web of murder now. But a joke like that can only last so long. Pretty soon things went sour again and they had to go back out on the street and look for something else to tide them over. The whole town was afraid of sundown because of what they did. You could hear crickets chirping and hopping just outside the lit-up gas station on the outskirts, outside the circle of light, somewhere deep in the vast unknown blackness of slithering live things surrounding the gentle townsfolk of Laughingly Lovably. The whole premises always lit up, the gas stations, the merchandise marts, private houses, restaurants and also the diners. Every branch of every tree now hung with brilliant lights all through this town. All the sidewalks and driveways were made of lit panels.

That old dog head kept lying there, one eye winking on and off like a burned-out bulb and flies swarming around. This is still last week I'm talking about. Would a licensed physician or animal control expert ever show up? No one knew. That was the wonderful thing about life in that broken down city. Everyone had already been eaten by something or several different things. Digested even but never fully swallowed. None of them. They all danced around, going to parties and the like, they kept having their fun. Life was beautiful for them. In the end Sam went out onto the street and packed it up in a paper sack. He was getting ready to throw it away when a hungry Rat-Eyes who had just gotten back from another part of town came out from under the tarpaulin and caught sight of him. Rat-Eyes offered Sam ten bucks for the dog's head. saying he wanted to preserve the head for a science experiment he was doing. Rat-Eyes was on his way back trailed by a cloud of blood-fat, maddened flies when the two winos jumped out from behind a bus and clubbed him. "Damn!" said Wino #2. "I thought that kid had a hamburger!" Laughing, he threw away the dog-head. Rat-Eyes came to a few hours later and crawled off into the distance. Blocks away, Sam folded his binoculars and opened another beer. The way he had it figured, as long as he kept on digging that hole in his backyard, there would always be a small imaginary way out.

Toys

He passed me, waving a fist
from a truck window, and soon looked
like a child driving a wheeled toy.
Traffic swallowed him and by now
he's a county away. Maybe there's
nothing more real than distance
though I sleep fitfully, even
on my uncratered street. Surely,
once a soft voice enthralled me.
A face drew near and filled up
the horizon. Today's story?
We migrate to work, migrate
from spouse to spouse, shore
to distant shore along such
raveling paths, in so many
small dubious vehicles

Michael Lauchlan

The Oath

We slit our wrists to the side
and put them together
and you told me your father
had been murdered
as our lines crossed and nothing
internal knew no boundaries.
We didn't die like I thought we would
and you spread our blood around your face
like war paint,
two checks under your brown eyes.
I tuned my guitar
and you danced naked
like a shaman
while I strummed an old folk song.
My parents were looking for a second house
in Florida
and I forgot to feed my mom's fish
and the dogs thought we were insane
but we were happy.
And in the kitchen
we laid down
like we owned the floor.
And we bled together on my mom's new tile
like love
burrowing into the earth.

When I see a pair of ducks
flying together to the ends of the map
I think of you, the one who gave me
more than her heart,
the one who
opened herself up.
And even though we didn't make it
to the end of the earth
I slept well and
I woke up in a better world.

Scott Laudati

Working Class

Last night, after my shift, I went to a poetry reading at the college. I love poets, the tender old heads who've paid attention to their entire lives, in spirit if not exactly in order. Poems about New Mexican copper mines, cellists in Sarajevo, and meteor showers up by Knoxville.

When it was over, after audience questions and the poets' answers that erupted in slow motion and hardened into new poems, I slipped from that reading room and across the twinkling campus to my car.

I stopped at the 24-hour Walgreens on the way back to my apartment. I was out of deodorant. Nearly out of toilet paper. I bought new razors and saddle soap for my work boots.

I fell asleep on the couch again while the neighbors, lovers, wrung new poison out of old words and splashed it across their walls.

Paul Luikart

Everything the Moon is Not

it is not the swirling wind
playing in the sway of branches
of an oddly illuminated tree

waving its arms against your
bedroom window, scraping
the shadow from early morning's

underbelly

it is not the tiny shards of brokenness
that litter the lawn of a once
close relationship

it is not the comma between
earth and sky, separating
our thought from prayer

it is not the streetlight, silhouetting
two desperate lovers amidst an acrid
August night in a Kentucky rental

the smell of musk and sweat
rising in the pale, muffled
air of an unpromised tomorrow

it is not the strength it takes
to somehow keep you and I
together, when soft words are never

present to save what was
never enough

it is not the light of the almost dying
that glows from the edge of the
never promised

it is not the will of an absent god
you can't shine bright without
the darkness to hide the truth about

what you really are, it is just the moon
and tonight, everything underneath
its bright rage

glistens

Kevin D. LeMaster

The Many Things That Rage

In 2015, I weighed 110 lbs.
Once I almost punched the floor with my face after a slight cut
on my thumb while cutting some oranges.
Curses boomed out of my mouth through my shambled frame.
My father walked into the kitchen.
"A chair," I said, "bring me a chair."
"A chair?"
"I'm going to faint."
"You're kidding, right?"
I held onto the stove
"I'm not."
A rainbow exploded in my eyes. I saw the colorful particles
dance all around the kitchen.
"Here's the chair," I heard my father say.
I dropped, trying to control my breathing.
My father handed me a ball of cotton soaked in rubbing alcohol.
"You're killing yourself," he said.
"I'm fine."
I had my goal set at 100lbs. I would stop then,
or I would rage down to hell
10 lbs. at a time.

Giovanni Mangiante

April 14 is *Cake and Cunnilingus Day*

And my father's birthday. I suppose
I'll have to wait until December 8:
Pretend to Be a Time Traveler Day
to go back to some year he was alive
so I can ask if he'd agree with that.

I mean, even a stranger could surmise
from his size that he enjoyed his cake.
But close as we were, there were limits.

I imagine my mother would insist I set
my imaginary time travel machine dial
for any December 21: *Humbug Day!*

Or if she was in a rather saucy mood,
November 8: *Tongue Twister Day*
or August 6: *Wiggle Your Toes Day.*

"More like March 18," my sister would groan.
"*National Awkward Moments Day …*"

"Nah," my resurrected father would snap,
"Try February 16: *Do a Grouch a Favor Day!*"

"Yeah, Howard?" my mother might reply,
"well, I just might be out of town March 14:
Steak and BJ Day." Surprising everyone
since she always lived for the holidays.

I could imagine her threatening my father
if he keeps it up, he might not see her until
July 18: *Get Out of the Dog House Day.*

But most days of the year I do pretend
it's *Pretend to Be a Time Traveler Day*
so I can keep the dial set on December 12:
National Ding-a-ling Day. When we're
encouraged to reconnect with those
we haven't heard from in a while.

Michael Montlack

Choose **Your Own Adventure**

Like what if you had married that bearded Capricorn.
You'd be in Denver now. Watching that beard slowly gray.

Or maybe mending a rickety garden gate somewhere alone
in California, your faded Angels jersey muddy as your knuckles.

You might imagine that same yard with a modest in-ground pool
instead of the garden. Or imagine having convinced that Capricorn
to move with you to California. Even shave his beard.

Just for fun: Imagine him developing a disdain for Denver.
And attribute it to how much he loves you.

When that seems unrealistic, unleash the monster, the life where
you finally find the nerve to have an affair with your friend's partner.
Ending their marriage. And your friendship. Enough trauma
to make you run off to Denver with that Capricorn
despite your hesitation. And your disdain.

If it keeps coming back to him, imagine the version in which
you are the Capricorn.

And if that doesn't work, imagine still another,
where you don't garden or swim or watch baseball.

Hell, make it one where you're not even looking for love.
And never had the slightest interest in astrology.

Michael Montlack

Class

I went to summer school in Glendale the month
after Grandma's surgery. The June mornings
were overcast and cold. I made a friend in typing class,
a thin girl who wore tight skirts and thick eyeliner.

On breaks, we stood on the curb and smoked
cigarettes she'd filched from her father.
We didn't talk much. In my adult mind I see a girl
weighted with dark secrets, but for me that summer

she was a gentle companion. That month I explored
Grandpop's tool shed, found his stash of novels
with buxom redheads on the covers, handsome
couples kissing, stories about women with roseate

nipples. I made friends with the neighbor girls
who wore white nail polish and black eyeliner
in spider-leg-thin lines. They used the forbidden
double negative and words that Mother taught me

weren't words. These were the kind of girls
my mother grew up with, this was the kind
of neighborhood she finally got away from.

Tamara Madison

Margaret Johnson

Her short white hair
Is curled into question marks
On her weekly walk
To the library
Where she will talk
With the young man
At the reference desk
Who reminds her of her son,
A Marine Corps lieutenant
Killed in Vietnam
And buried in a row
Of white crosses
In Arlington Cemetery.
The obscenity of war,
The despicable repetition,
Has never left her,
The random and designed killing
She lives with, clenching
Her hands each time
The loss invades her,
Opening them
After a deep breath.

Michael Miller

Dream, with Fake Leonard Cohen Lyrics

Of course it was music that woke me up.
The dream ended with a needle lurching
      across a record that wasn't even in the dream.

I had been talking with Maya.
In the dream, her name was *Maya.*
Which seems deep, since *Maya* means *illusion* –
      except that it's the first name
      you'd pick if you were trying to sound deep,
      which means it's not terribly deep.

We had been sitting on her bed. There was an
      allusion to having sex, and we agreed:
we should have sex.
She asked me to pull off her pants.
I pulled off her pants.

Then, she said she needed to clean her yoga mat.
She couldn't find the 409 anywhere,
      and even though I had been gone from that house a long,
      long time, I knew it was under the bathroom sink.
The cabinet door opened the wrong way.
Still, I plucked out the 409.
Maya got to cleaning the hell out of that yoga mat.

I walked around straightening things to kill time,
      dipping into brand new rooms
      off the old hall.
I thought to myself how enlightened it was
      that we had simply been talking,
      and then agreed to have sex.
Sex, I thought, should always be like that:
      an unremarkable thing, no emotional temperature,
      a greeting between casual acquaintances –
      on the sidewalk, at work, at the grocery store, humdrum.
They should make a law making sex so.
I thought: there have been many poems
      that just up and say, *I am making it so.*
So. There you have it. I officially decree it here:

sex is, once again, no big deal.
Though poems have a poor legislative track record.

By then, Maya had finished cleaning her mat, but was stuck
      on the phone.
She was talking at length about her diagnosis,
      how nobody had ever practiced one harder.
I shuffled some more stuff around; decluttering, waiting.
I noticed several wooden schecks on the patio.
We had left them mowling enormously in the thickening twilight.
What will the neighbors think?
Fuck the neighbors.
Well, I thought – until they pass my new sex law, I can't.

I sat back down on Maya's bed, and waited.
In the heavily shellacked doorframe, she appeared.
I said, "I know this sounds really cliché, but …"

Maya finished the thought from inside me.
Maya said: *The heart –*

It beats you till you die, because
It always chooses life.

It opens like a vista.
It closes like a knife.

Joshua McGuire

Cerebellum

As a kid I thought *cerebellum* meant: a fancy kind of bell.
And even when I found out it didn't,
    the word still made sense.

Because a boxer who gets hit in the brain
    still gets his bell rung.
When you have an idea, it chimes in instantly – like a bell.
And the school librarian wore bell bottoms,
    scuttling brown around our cerebral afternoons.

I got older, and learned that *bella* meant beautiful.
I thought that cerebellum was beauty –
    thought thinking was pretty. It was indoor work,
    like some antebellum belle of the ball –

Though this thought showed me how *bellum* meant *war*.
And I came to see how the brain was, in fact, at war
    with itself – a house divided, a mind blown
    against the way things really are, alone.

Latin gave one last false clue: *ceres* meant *candles*.
Again, a cerebral image: flame equaling study,
    brain work in the pre-electric thicket.
The life of the mind was a *candle beauty*.

Or perhaps the brain was shaped like melted wax.

Then I googled it.
Bellum is a diminutive: *cerebellum* means *little brain*.
The cerebellum doesn't even do any thinking.
It's mostly just muscle control, and balance.

So, cerebellum: the war for beauty and light
    was never anything more
    than a hand, an arm, showing up
    at the right place, in the right time.

Joshua McGuire

After Fukushima

Radioactive rain clatters the alley, fine gravel, tips of cold
fingered children slide against my scalp and through my hair like
a child's curiosity: insistent, observant with wonder but without
love. Did you ever

touch my hair with loose fingers? I can't remember how you
loved me, only that you did. Mother, what a world you bore me
into. Daffodils spring elated through the earth for you, but you
turned on your heel. Left as you meant to do decades before
when the world turned

to particles of dust and fire and its violence reached a terrible
precedent. A child's fingers grasp at the past and in the past
beyond that, a boy observant with what would become a
dangerous will and curiosity touched with cool fingers crystals,
minerals, their scintillating layers and colors, textures and
formations.

But it wasn't enough.

Next came a fascination with sulphur, copper, magnesite.
Chemical compounds, gases amorphous, indefinite between
cellular structure. What is the essence of life? What heavens
exist beyond the limited eye?

There are those who believe man should have no limits. The
appetite for more, atoms of greed for understanding, manifest an
insatiable desire to know, and the power to wield it.

The boy cannot be stopped.

No one told him, "Enough." Because we do not know what
enough is. What will fill the void of our insecurity – this
knowledge that we bleed a red which turns to rust, we are mortal,
and we die? Is it spite at God that has made us thus?

The boy picks and examines with fingers and fingernails pulling apart all that he would know – with microscopes and refractors, precise cold instruments brilliant and elegant but without love and no presentiment of remorse –

the atom is split. Caesium 137, iodine 131 – and light, light, glorious light sears our eyes and Icarus falls –

Mother, in your time all this came to be. Yet you had me anyway, fed me, clothed me taught me how to plant daffodil bulbs deep in the soil of a red clay pot and how to wait. And wait.

You never returned.

Left me listening
to the dubious rain
clattery and cold
with its hydrogen and oxygen
caesium 137
        strontium 90

Left me with too many questions and a love of words
and beauty
taught me the meaning of choice, its blade edge
of devastation

its free fall

of joy

Lisa Marguerite Mora

Sean Padraic McCarthy

The Veil

Melissa O'Shea closed all the blinds. She pulled her blouse over her head and unsnapped her bra. And then she pushed her shorts – they used to be much tighter but she had lost twenty-five pounds these last few months – down over her hips. Shook them free from her foot and sent them sailing across the room, and then she slipped out of her panties, brand new and pretty with bright blue flowers, and left them on the floor. She had bought the panties for Scott. She wanted everything new for him. She ran the tips of her fingers over the top of the bristles of the smudge stick. It felt, looked, like a small old broom, bound tight in the middle with dark twine; she had bought it in Salem just the week before.

Her friend, Harriet, who had gone with her to Salem had suggested she get one as something of a lark, but then Melissa, laughing, thought about it a little and decided to give it a shot, that it just might work. She wanted Ronan out of here, and she wanted him out now.

Melissa O'Shea wasn't of Irish descent – she was of Polish – but Ronan was Irish, as had been her first husband, Dave, and her boyfriend Scott before that. Now Scott was her boyfriend again when he wasn't being married, and Melissa was in love with him and couldn't be happier. Except for when she thought about his wife, who was a bitch, and trying to ruin everything. And except for Ronan. Ronan who wouldn't get the fuck out. He was gone physically – moved the next town over – but he was still here. She could feel him here. Smell him. And she wanted him gone.

The witch in the store in Salem was probably crazy but she had really looked like a witch. A thick head of long black hair. A black dress and a big fat ass. Melissa's ass had never been fat but it had been fatter than it was now, and she was never going back to that. Anyway, the witch had told her that this time or year the veil between this world and the next, the past and the present, the living and the dead, was thinnest and that the smudge stick should work in getting Ronan out – that it could be used for spirits that weren't yet dead – and all the negative energy he had built up for so many years in this room. It was important to get him out of the house completely because she wanted Scott in; and he would be in, as soon as he left *Sheila* – even just the name made Melissa want to vomit. In any case, she had to start smudging somewhere, and she and Ronan had spent most of their time alone together – time without the kids, Kacie and Lizzie – in this room. And then Ronan had accused her of cheating, but she told him it couldn't be cheating because it wasn't really cheating if you were in love with the other person, had always been in love with them even though you hadn't even known it, and you didn't love your spouse anymore. Then it wasn't cheating, and she hated it when he said it was cheating. She hated cheaters. She had always been firm on that. Clear. Cheaters were awful. And Melissa wasn't a cheater.

She just wanted Ronan gone. Gone from her memory. Gone from this house. And then she could be happy. Finally happy. She had waited too many years, her whole life, to finally be happy. The girls had always been attached to Ronan, and they hadn't been happy with her since she kicked him out, but they would get used to it. Scott was a wonderful man, a better man, and they would see that. And besides, they wouldn't be in the house for too much longer anyway, and then she and Scott could be alone. Happy. The way it should have been from the beginning.

Melissa looked towards the door that opened up onto the top deck. She had frosted over the windows so no one could see inside. But she could just picture him, Ronan sneaking up here at night. Trying to peek in. Spying.

Asshole.

She listened a moment. Nothing. And then she flicked her lighter; she smoked a little pot up here now, just a little to help her sleep, to calm her nerves, and the lighter came in handy. The tip of the smudge had just started to burn when she turned to bathroom. The light was on in the bathroom.

And Ronan stood there.

Melissa almost screamed.

But then he just smiled at her.

And then he was gone. Turning transparent and the quickly fading.

Melissa's hands were shaking.

Fucking asshole, she thought. *Asshole, asshole, asshole ...*

She held the lighter to the end of the stick again, and waited until it had fully caught. Ashes sparked a little, and floated to the floor, and Melissa began to circle her way about the room, holding the stick high above her head.

There was a time when she never would have done anything like this. She was Catholic. A good Catholic. When she was little she sometimes fantasized about being a nun one day – cloistered and clean, or maybe out in the community, helping the miserable, the sick and the abused. Mother Teresa had been her idol, and the day she was beatified, Melissa had gone to the empty church and spent the afternoon silently praying amongst the candles and the darkness, praying for them all.

Now Melissa hadn't been to church in almost a year. She used to go to church with Ronan and the girls every week. Not just Christmas. Not just holidays. Not just Palm Sunday and Easter. Every fucking week. She wasn't a hypocrite. She had never been a hypocrite. And that was why once Ronan accused her of cheating with Scott, she had stopped going to church. Right then and there. Ronan was holier than though – just like her mother – so he kept going to church even though they were practically divorced. Talking all his bullshit. She hated him. None of this would have happened to begin with. If it weren't for him. If he weren't so self-absorbed. If he had been more attentive.

The entire room was covered in dust. The headboard, the bureau, the television and the cabinet it was in. Her jewelry. The ceiling fan. The pictures. And the floor …

She never remembered the floor getting covered with dust like this, like it was perpetually undisturbed. And these days, that was almost true. She didn't allow anyone in here since Ronan had moved out. Well, except Scott once or twice when he had snuck in from the top deck and they had sex before he went running off into the night again. No, now she kept the doors locked, and the girls out. The girls were eighteen and sixteen and she loved them, but she had had enough of being a mother, and she didn't completely trust them, didn't know what they might go back and tell Ronan if they saw anything in here. Letters from Scott. Pictures. She kept a picture of Scott on her bureau, surrounded by candles, and in the picture he was standing on the beach and whipping the photographer the finger. That was a little juvenile, but that was okay, he could be juvenile; it didn't matter. She was fucking in love with him again and nothing else mattered.

Now she noticed what looked to be footprints in the dust on the floor. Big footprints. Or bigger than hers at least. And she wondered if Ronan *really* had somehow got up here. Snooping around. Looking for evidence to use in the divorce. The footprints suddenly began to multiply – running all over the floor, as if in fact someone were in the room with her now, and Melissa stepped cautiously back and stood with her shoulders tense and her back tight to the door to the deck. Chin up and eyes lowered. The footprints ran about in circles in the dust, and Melissa reached cautiously over, not taking her eyes away from what she was seeing, and flicked the switch to the ceiling fan.

The fan spun into the life, full speed, and then the dust was swirling and the footsteps were rising. Still running about, but rising. Just for a moment. And then they dissipated, breaking apart like sunbeams in the light coming through the blinds on the window. Melissa clicked off the ceiling fan, and the dust of the footsteps settled back to the floor. Gone. Untraceable. To most people. But not to Melissa. She had seen them.

Fucking Ronan. It had to be Ronan.

She just wanted him gone.

She wished she could erase the past. Erase everything back until she was first with Scott. Seventeen. In love. And then she would be happy.

Melissa took a deep breath, waited again a moment for something to happen. Something. Anything. And then when nothing did, she relit the smudge stick and began to whisper the chant the witch had taught her:

Spirit or man
Flesh or wind
Hear these words
And away you will spin
The past is gone
The past cannot be
And with cedar and sage
I exorcise thee!

Ronan now lived now ten minutes down the road, but still too close. After twenty years of marriage, it had taken her six friggin months to get him to physically leave. She had been beside herself. What self-respecting man would stay around the house after his wife told him she wanted a divorce? After his wife had made it clear that he was not wanted? She had told him in March, the day after she had first seen Scott again, physically, and he hadn't left until September. It was crazy. All she wanted to do was see Scott, and all Ronan had done was get in the way. Asking questions and making accusations, watching her all the time.

And he was still watching her, she was sure of it. And the energy he had left needed to be smudged. She didn't belong to him; she belonged to Scott, and Ronan couldn't see that. She had always belonged to Scott – she just hadn't been aware, at least not until they had connected on Facebook, and he told her, explained it to her – she had always been his number one. Always, he said.

"But how can it be always?" she had whispered to him on the phone. "We broke up twenty-five years ago. We didn't see or speak to each other for twenty-five years. We broke up, and you got married. You're still married. To Sheila."

And Scott on the other end of the line had hesitated a moment, and then taken a breath. "We never broke up."

"We didn't?" Melissa had asked. She didn't understand, but his words had her intrigued, and she wanted to listen.

"No," he said. "We didn't."

"But we're both married, to someone else. How could we not have broken up?"

"You said you sent me a letter back then, right?"

"I did."

"A letter telling me you were breaking up with me?"

"I did."

"Well, I never received it. So if I never received it, then I couldn't have read it, and if I didn't read it, you didn't break up with me because I didn't know that's what you were doing."

"You didn't know?"

"No. And if I never received it, we never broke up. I work for the Post Office, so believe me, I know – if people don't receive things, they can't read them."

So there it was. It dawned on her right there and then; he was absolutely right. And since he was right, and they had never broken up, then being with him wouldn't be cheating even if she were still married to Ronan. She hated cheaters.

Ronan appeared in the bathroom again, and Melissa again rushed over and pulled the door shut. The room was now full of smudge smoke, so it shouldn't be long. She hoped. Soon he would be gone.

And then she could work on getting Scott back for good, full time. No more Sheila. Melissa would smudge her, too, if she had to. Of course, she was well aware that all the smudging could maybe stir up some problems. And she had enough problems. She didn't want to stir up any more. And she didn't want to piss off Mrs. Griffin. Not again. Mrs. Griffin was the old lady who had lived here before them and died on the living room floor, heart attack, and every time Melissa moved stuff around, or they put on an addition, or knocked down a wall, she started acting up. Knocking things off tables and shelves, and whispering in darkness. And always the footsteps moving about upstairs. No, Melissa didn't need her involved.

Melissa repeated the chant again, and began to pace about the room, the stick held high above her head. She could see nothing, the room was so full of smoke, and then she heard coughing. Coughing coming from the room next door, the girls' room. Coughing, and then a voice, saying something cryptic and distant, too far for Melissa to hear. The girls? The girls weren't supposed to be home yet, and if they were home, she was going to kill them. She ran to the door and swung it open.

But it wasn't the girls.

It was a woman. A small, old lady. Crooked, and covered with black spots and mold, like the branch of an old cherry tree. She reached for Melissa, and Melissa screamed and threw the smudge at her. She swung shut the door, and then ran through the room – but now, somehow, the room was fading, the furniture gone, and the floor, dropping, nothing but smoke – towards the back stairs.

Mrs. Griffin was in the girls' room, she thought. Melissa had heard her before, but never seen her – although Kacie as small child said she used to see her, that the "old lady" used to sing to her – and now she was there. What had Melissa done? The smudge, it had to be the smudge. The goddamn thing must've backfired, twisted things up. Fucking smudge. She never should have listened to Harriet, and that fat old witch in Salem.

Melissa hurried down the back stairs, terrified to look back, and then when she got to the bottom, the living room, she came to a sudden stop.

A man stood in the kitchen, his back to her. But it wasn't her kitchen. Not her kitchen now. It looked like her old kitchen. Her first apartment. And the man ... from behind ... looked like her first husband. Dave.

He turned to look at her, holding a butter knife – he was buttering toast. Black sneakers and dress shorts and white socks pulled up to his knees, hair combed back like he thought he was a movie star. Thin long lips, and a ski slope nose. Dark eyes, that sarcastic glint to them. It was him. Dave. Except he was still young. And now he had something on his right leg, tucked into his sock. And it looked like a tail ...

He looked her up and down. "Hey, where's the clothes? You feeling frisky, Gladys?" Gladys. That had been his nickname for her, he called her Gladys. She couldn't remember why. And the sight of him brought back the old, familiar nausea. And even from here, she believed she could smell him. Part Polo cologne, part vomit.

"I'd say you're going to get me all horny," he said, "but I think your mother is coming by in a few minutes, and what's that old bitch going to say if she comes in and sees me doing you doggie? Or even just sees you running around naked?"

Melissa looked herself up and down. Naked. She was still naked. She wrapped her arms around her chest. She was definitely hallucinating now, had to be. She had heard stuff before, voices – who didn't? – but nothing like this. Unless she was dreaming. She could be dreaming. And what the fuck was he doing here? She hadn't seen him in over twenty years. Hadn't smelled him. Not since the last day in court. He lived in Kentucky or something now. Right at home in redneck land. Probably beating women right out in the open down there, and getting away with it. His favorite thing was body shots she remembered though, punches to the gut. No marks, no questions. But then every now and then he would slip. Coldcock her. She still had the police photos – one side of her face black and blue and double the size of the other. And she still had a scar above her lip.

Fucking loser.

She hated him. Still. The hate was old, but just the sight of him made it feel brand spanking new.

"What the fuck are you doing here?" she said to him. "I don't want you here. Either get out of my house or I'm going to call the cops. Just like the old days, Dave."

"These are the good old days, Gladys." He chuckled. That sarcastic, cynical little chuckle. She hated that chuckle. He went back to buttering his toast. "And what are you going to call them about now? What are you going to tell them? I live here. I'm like a victim in my own home. You're always trying to get me in trouble for something. I think we could be so happy, I always thought we could be happy – like wicked happy – if you just listened to me. And weren't such a bitch."

"I was never happy with you," she snapped. "I was miserable with you."

He giggled. "Oh, you were happy sometimes. Remember that night with the hot fudge and whip cream? Once I hit that G spot, your body was bucking like a bronco on the bed. And you were happy, believe me."

Melissa looked around the room. It was all here. The ugly purple couch – he picked out the couch, he picked out everything, controlled everything – and the candelabra on the dining room table. It showed they had class, she remembered him saying. Their old stereo, cassette player and turntable in the corner. The framed painting – flowers spilling out of a cornucopia, and the drawing of the two of them he had an artist draw in Provincetown. Melissa with her head on his shoulder. Now she was going to be sick, she was sure of it.

"You want some toast?" he asked her.

The wind suddenly picked up outside, boxes and newspapers tumbling down the street, a shower of leaves racing by the window. The wind was loud and rattling the glass.

Melissa saw feet, shoes, pass by the front window, descending from the sky. Footsteps on the porch, and then the doorbell. She swung open the door. And he was right. She was there. Her mother. Empty eyes. Eyes like glass. A doll's eyes. Her hair piled high on top of her head like it was nineteen sixty-five – her mother kept that hairstyle right into the nineties, long after she had stopped fucking the family pediatrician – an she had an umbrella in hand like she thought she was Mary Poppins or something. Melissa hadn't talked to her mother in six years. Now the woman folded the umbrella, poked the end at Melissa's navel.

"Going to a party?" her mother asked. You never stop, do you? Fuck, fuck, fuck, sex, sex, sex. I'll still pray for you dear." Her mother pushed by her, and Melissa stood gazing in amazement. Outside was her old street. Bartelby St., Brockton. A small box like blue Corolla with a rusted fender was parked near the curb. Broken porches and trash in the yards smothered in tall grass. Dogs barking and children crying. She hated Brockton. The only thing off, different, was the colors. The colors were nearly blinding.

Reds and blues and greens and yellow, each one a little brighter than the other, swirling like a Van Gogh canvas, pulsing. Melissa slammed shut the door. She grabbed a blanket off the couch and wrapped it around her.

Her mother, Barbara, put her purse on the table, and then marched over towards Dave. For a second Melissa believed, watching the determination in her mother's step, that she was going to smack him. But she didn't. She kissed him. A prolonged – much too long – kiss on the lips, and then Dave returned to his buttering task. Her mother smacked her lips. "Mmmmwah!"

It made no sense. Her mother hated Dave. Always hated Dave, and hated him more each year until he was gone. Dave was the reason Melissa and her mother had their first falling out. Or maybe it was their second, maybe Scott caused the first – she couldn't keep track anymore; countless falling outs.

"If you don't give your man what he wants, then someone else is going to dear," Barbara suddenly said, her eyes so empty that for a moment Melissa feared she might get sucked right in. Black holes.

"But you hate him," Melissa said, "you always said he was the biggest asshole on the planet. That was your nickname for him – 'asshole.'"

Charlotte's mouth went slack, silent for a moment – the silence and look which usually foretold, preceded, the lie, whatever it might be. She needed a few seconds to conjure it, but Barbara was one of the most prolific liars Melissa had ever encountered, and she was usually fairly quick. "That hatchet was buried a long time ago, dear. Besides, all men are assholes, you know that – they can't help it. And sometimes 'asshole' can be a term of endearment."

"Your daughter is the queen of nasty names," Dave said then. "You should hear some of the things she calls me. Terrible. It's just terrible. I'm not abusive. She's the one who is abusive, I always tell her that. Terrible."

"Oh, she says terrible things to everybody," said Barbara, "no brain to mouth filter. Doesn't care what she says to anybody, who she hurts. Just thinks of herself. Selfish. She's always been incredibly selfish. I

96

tried to explain that to the other husband – the second one – but he wouldn't listen. Moron, that's my name for him – Moron."

"Second husband?" asked Dave. He still had a little smirk on his face, looking amused. "Melissa has a second husband?"

Barbara took a deep breath, exhaled. Dramatic. "Yes. The problem with Melissa is that she's a little slut. Always been a slut. Ever since she's been old enough to … old enough to …" Barbara wiggled her fingers in the air, "start touching herself. In with the fingers, all day long."

Melissa could feel her rage simmering, and she fought back her tears. "That's not true. How can you say that? I'm your daughter."

Barbara looked at Dave sideways. "Are you?" she said to Melissa. "Who really knows anymore. I've had so many I've lost track. Besides, sluts are sluts. It is what it is."

Melissa was crying now. "You're the one who used to fuck Dr. Petrius."

"I never did any such thing." She turned to Dave again. "Melissa lies a lot, too. Can't help herself. It's, it's … what's the word."

"Pathological," Dave said.

"That's right," said Barbara. "Pathological. It's pathological. And she hurt the whole family, over and over. Still does."

"How many kids do you have, Barbara?" Dave asked then.

Barbara paused. "Eighteen. I had eighteen children."

"That's a lie," shouted Melissa. "You never had eighteen children. You had seven."

"Eleven of them died, dear. Monster babies, a few premature. I had two sets of twins, one set of triplets, all stillborn. You almost died yourself, you were breech. They said you lost a lot of oxygen. It was terrible."

"You lie," Melissa whispered, "You're a liar." She just wanted them both out. Wanted her house back, this apartment gone. She wondered if she could wish them away. Smudge them. She could go back upstairs, get the smudge. But then she turned and the entrance to the stairway was gone. The stairs were gone.

"It's only a lie if you don't believe it yourself, dear," her mother said, "It doesn't matter what other people believe."

"Is that all it takes?" A man's voice, in the next room over. Off stage, thought Melissa. It sounded off stage. But of course it was off stage, it had to be off stage.

The voice was her father's. And her father was dead.

Barbara just raised her eyebrows quick, coy. "Asshole," she whispered.

Melissa felt her soul leave her body, everything leave her body. She couldn't move. Her father was in next room. She wanted to see him, she missed him terribly, but she was terrified to see him. Both Dave and her mother were silent now, staring at her. Melissa dropped the blanket, naked again, and stepped past them. She started down the hall, shadows closing in behind her, and when she turned, everything was gone, everything gray. Fading. A fog, creeping slowly. The smudge stick? She wondered if she stopped, waited, if she would disappear, too.

But she didn't want to learn. Didn't want to disappear. Stuck in that apartment with the two of them. Her tormenters. They had ruined her life, both of them. She hated them.

The noise still came from ahead. It sounded like a television.

And it was. The first thing Melissa saw when she turned the corner. A big box TV. And a black and white image on the screen. John Wayne, an older John Wayne. Big Belly, and his thumbs looped through his gun belt. Hat at an angle, and patch over one eye.

"The Duke," her father said. "Rooster Cogburn. His best ones were his last ones. We should all have such a closing act, little girl." Her father looked frail, white T-shirt and raggedy brown bathrobe. But it was definitely him. Wild gray hair, a Roman nose, and hesitant, searching eyes. Blue eyes. Or eye, she suddenly thought. He was wearing an eye patch, too. Why was he wearing an eye patch? He never wore an eye patch.

"I lost one in the ground," he suddenly said. "It was terrible. It's tough to find things in the dark. And it's really dark, Melissa. Really dark. Do you want to see?"

Melissa shook her head. "No."

Her father turned back to the television. The room was the room off the kitchen at her mother's house. Her father always sat in there while he watched TV, especially as he waited to die. She could see the black, pot-bellied woodstove, and the baskets on the walls in the living room beyond. A cuckoo clock, and picture of Jesus, eyes loving but sad, as he opened his robe and exposed his heart. A picture of the blessed mother. coddling the baby Christ in her arms. The sun beams dancing in the light coming in through the windows, and everywhere dust.

And suddenly her father was covered in dust, too.

"Ashes to ashes," he said.

"I miss you," she whispered, and she started to cry. "I love you." He was the only one who understood her, the only one. Gave her space, knew her temper – the same as his – let her vent. And then moved on. They both always moved on. Let it out, and then move on. He understood that. The only one.

"I love you, too, little girl," he said.

Melissa looked at the enormous oxygen tank beside him, standing at forty-five degree angle in its stand, thick, rubber wheels. The tubes, and his nose pieces, lay draped over the arm of the chair.

"Why aren't you wearing your oxygen?" she asked.

Her father looked right, then looked left, then looked right back at her. "Why do you think? Because I'm dead. What would I need oxygen for? Why aren't you wearing any clothes?"

Melissa glanced down, suddenly mortified again. Still naked. Her father hadn't seen her naked since she was small. Nobody had. Except Dave, and Ronan, and Scott. She loved Scott, and now often wore her bikini for him while hanging around his apartment. He liked to watch her cook for him, and clean up, while in her bikini. Sometimes naked. He liked that, he said. But now, she noticed, her pubic hair was back. It had been gone for months, since she got back with Scott, since he had told her he preferred everything shaved clean, no body hair, none. So off it had gone – she had never fully shaved down there, but now everybody did, so why not? Why shouldn't she? But now it was back. Had it been back in the kitchen, with her mother, and Dave? She wasn't sure.

"I left them upstairs." She felt her face flush. She reached for a pillow on the couch, held it out in front her. "And now I can't get back there. I was smudging, and the witch said you are supposed to be naked, free, when you smudge for it to work."

"Free?"

"From all earthly possessions," she said quietly. "Just your body. And your soul."

"What were you trying to smudge?"

"Ronan," she said, "The past. But it must not have worked."

"Why do you say that?"

"Because this is the past."

"Is it?" he asked. And again he was smiling. But the dust atop him was thicker now, coating his eyelashes. The dust atop everything was thicker. And then the furniture beneath it, began to crumble, collapsing in on itself. As did her father. Melissa let out a small cry, and closed her eyes, and when she opened them again, there was nothing. Just an empty room, an empty void, and a blanket of dust. Her father gone.

And then she noticed a small rounded door appeared on the far wall, just big enough for her to crawl through. And there was a conversation taking place on the other side.

Small voices, coming from far away, echoing.

For a moment, Melissa thought she recognized the voices. They sounded like the girls, Kacie and Lizzie, but the voices weren't 18 and

16. Maybe 5 and 3. Maybe younger. And the small door was now the only way out of the room.

Melissa crouched down and opened the door, and her face was warmed with a rush of stale air. Inside the doorway was a dark tunnel smelling of insulation and dust, everything dry, and the voices now while still present somehow sounded even further away. There were toys just inside the tunnel, dolls – baby dolls and Barbie dolls, a trail of them – and most of them were half dressed or naked. One Barbie missing a leg, and another infant doll's eye had gone weak, wouldn't stay open, as if she were winking. Melissa pushed the dolls the aside, cursing under her breath, and then she began to crawl. The tunnel seemed to be growing smaller, tighter, as she made her way along, but strangely enough so did Melissa.

Melissa began to feel claustrophobic, and almost turned back, but behind her, through the round little door now, too, far in the distance, someone was crying, sounding like Melissa herself, and someone was screaming. A dish shattered, and then the slap of a hand on skin. Dave. And then someone cried out, and the cry sounded like her mother's. No, she couldn't go back. Dave was still back there, her mother was back there.

She crawled ten paces forward, and when she looked to her right, there was glass, the lights like stage lights behind it, and illuminated beneath the light there was a picture, but it wasn't a picture, it was people, but not real people. The people looked like the wax figures you see in museums. And one was Melissa.

It was their back yard. The above ground pool. The wooden swing set that had taken Ronan something ridiculous, like three weeks, to put together. And the girls were there, and the girls were small. Frozen still as they ran across the lawn, the grass bright green. Melissa was on her knees in the garden beneath the back deck, small shovel in hand, her head raised as she watched the girls, keeping an eye on them, making sure they were safe.

Melissa kept crawling.

The next was a scene from their wedding, hers and Ronan's. Dancing, Melissa with her chin on his shoulder. And in the one after that Melissa was dressed in her graduation cap and gown, blue, high school, smiling wide, and holding the cap tight to her head. Her friends were beside her. Paul – tall and gangly with tinted glasses – had a cigarette dangling from his lips, and was giving the peace sign. 1991, she thought. The girl on the other side of her was Muriel, round and soft and sweet. Melissa had once thought she had a crush on her beyond her friendship, and they had kissed once.

She kept crawling.

Through the next window she could see a Christmas scene. Her grandmother's house. The room was packed with people, mostly children, and the tall tree stood by the front window. Her brother Phillip, slim still, and looking to be in his teens, stood by the tree a present in hand, smiling wide and glass eyes, and looking as if … he could see her. But he couldn't see her – he wasn't real, not here, wasn't moving. Wasn't alive. Her father sat on the steps, hands folded between his knees, he, too, younger. And her younger siblings – Kevin, Sandy, and Robbie, dressed in Christmas red, and not possibly older than 9, and 7, and 6. Sandy had a large bow in her hair, and Melissa's grandmother, the matriarch, now five years dead, sat in the chair in the corner. Skin still translucent, and eyes red rimmed and watery. Watching everything carefully. Cigarette in hand.

"We come from a long line of Catholics," she had once told Melissa. "And then the Catholics mixed with the gypsies, and see what you get, Melissa? See what you get? You should be ashamed of yourself. You. Your mother told me everything. Pulling down your pants the way you do. Early and often, for all the boys in the neighborhood? Ashamed, the grandmother had said. Your mother was right. You should ashamed.

And Melissa had forgotten about that. Until now. She had forgotten about a lot of things.

But they were all there. Inside the glass case. Her whole family.

My mother said,
that I never should,
play with gypsies in the woods.

The words, the old nursery rhyme, whispered through her head as if brought there on a breeze. The singing voices of children.

Old children, she thought. Long dead.

Melissa kept crawling. She passed several more scenes. Her first car – a battered Fiat, the bumper held up with duct tape. The attic of their house with the dirt yard, holes in the roof and bats flying in. Melissa on the floor, beneath a sleeping bag. With Scott. She paused a moment longer on that one, her heart stuttering. With Scott. She had her head on his chest, and he was smoking a cigarette, staring at the ceiling, the bats. Suspended in time.

The next display was of the outdoors. Green grass and a sandbox. A towering oak tree painted on the background in the distance. Melissa now not older than three or four sat in a sandbox with her friend Cindy Cummings. Melissa wore her yellow polka-dot bikini – just like the song, she remembered, she used to sing the song when she wore the bikini – and she, cross-legged, was pulling the bottoms aside to show

Cindy something. And her mother was coming out the door, rushing – a look of horror, a look of rage, and the long cutting board she used to beat them in hand.

Melissa felt the tears welling up inside her again. She moved on, and there in the last display, right before the small door with light coming through from beneath, sat a man. Late middle age. Slick black hair, a pompadour, and swollen red nose. Thick opaque glasses magnifying his eyes. His belly big and white, and his pants down around his ankles, his erection in hand. The man from the couch.

The couch.

Melissa leapt back, landing on her bottom in the tunnel. She felt a trickle of sweat move down her side.

She hadn't seen him in years, and even now she wasn't completely sure whom he was, whom he had been. It was too long ago, she was too small. And she sometimes saw him in dreams, and sometimes in fleeting memories. Heard his voice, wet and hoarse. Surreal. Few words, flashing images. People without faces. Never looking this real. Not since then, when he was.

Babysitting. The smaller children sleeping, and Melissa and her brother Phillip with him, barely in grade school, on the couch. Her clothes and Phillip's in a small pile on the floor.

It was all for fun, she remembered the man saying, laughing. Everybody was having fun.

The display case began to darken, the man going gray, mixing, and then the lights were out and he was gone. And once again Melissa was alone in the tunnel. Darkness. She crawled a few more feet, and she reached another small door. The voices still coming from the other side, still echoing, but closer. More real.

They were talking about a doll. Baby Lovey.

Baby Lovey. Melissa hesitated a moment. She knew that name.

She knocked twice, and then the voices on the other side quieted. One shushed the other, and then whispered. They waited. And Melissa knocked again. She heard a scamper of feet, and then one of them began to cry – the voice sounded as if she couldn't have been older than two – and then the other shushed her again.

Melissa lifted the latch and pushed open the door. The light was suddenly bright, flooding in the upon the tunnel. She was looking at two little girls. Probably four and two.

Kacie. And Lizzie.

They were at the far end of the room, away from the tunnel door, by the window overlooking the street – but there didn't look to be a street outside. No trees. Just a deep blue. Kacie held a raggedy looking little doll – hair in braids and one eye lazy, Louie, Melissa thought – in her hand, and a naked Barbie in the other. And Lizzie held an infant baby doll in a clown suit, purple marker scribbled across her face.

Baby Lovey.

Kacie looked at Lizzie – Lizzie had stopped crying – and then at Melissa.

"Are you a ghost?" Kacie asked.

Melissa shook her head. "No, of course not silly."

The girls just stared at her.

"I'm your mother," Melissa said.

Kacie and Lizzie both turned and looked at each other, silent, and then back at Melissa.

"Where are your clothes little girl?" Kacie said.

Melissa looked down to see she was still naked, but now covered with dust, cobwebs. Dirt on her knees. And she supposed she did look a little like a ghost.

"Lizzie is these babies' mommy," Kacie said. "She's a good mommy."

Melissa glanced around the room. The floor was lined with dozens of dolls. One long neat row. Some Barbie dolls. Brat dolls. Baby Dolls. And a couple American girl dolls, she remembered buying; the girls had loved the American girl dolls. Now all lay in repose, small pillows under their heads, and blankets over their bodies. Tucked in.

Lizzie popped a binky back in her mouth. She then went to the bed against the far wall, picked up a knitted blanket, toddled over and handed it to Melissa. Melissa took the blanket.

"Now you won't be cold little girl," Kacie said.

Melissa wrapped the blanket around her. The room was full of things she hadn't seen, hadn't thought of, in years. The Winnie the Pooh night light, the two beds she and Ronan had picked up at a yard sale, and then Melissa had painted white. A mobile hanging from the ceiling that Ronan had bought Kacie at a shop down in Martha's Vineyard – the cow jumping over the moon. Kacie had loved cows – loved to stop at the local dairy to see them – and she had loved the moon. There were two red, stuffed, Elmo chairs, and the Cinderella television, the sound down, playing *Blues Clues*. But the television had no chord.

"I'm glad to see you guys are keeping your room clean," Melissa said. She remembered the days of cleaning the room. Her rage. Screaming. Pointing her finger, directing. And Lizzie toddling back and forth, picking toys, dolls, up off the floor and methodically putting them in their toy box. Two, Melissa thought. She was two then, too. A baby. So why the rage, why had she screamed?

"Lizzie's a good cleaner," Kacie said now. "I'm a good messer."

"Well, I hope you help her clean, too," Melissa said.

"Well, sometimes," said Kacie. "And sometimes the old lady helps, too." Kacie pointed at the empty rocking chair in the corner. The one Ronan used to use to rock them, the nightly songs. "Puff the Magic Dragon." "Raindrops Keep Falling on My Head." And "Taxi."

"Taxi," Melissa thought. She hadn't heard that song in years.

Lizzie toddled over and picked up a small baby bottle, held it before the lips of a doll on the floor. "That baby's hungry," Kacie said. "Lizzie's a good mommy."

Kacie then went to the small white bureau, one drawer broken and hanging at an angle, and reached in and pulled out a small blue dress. She walked over and handed the dress to Melissa. "You should put this on, so you won't be cold and won't be naked."

"That won't fit me, silly," Melissa said.

But Kacie just stared. "It will fit you. Everything fits. Here."

Melissa looked down at her legs again, at her whole body. She glanced towards the mirror on the far side of the room, and then felt her heart seized up again. She was small again. It wasn't possible. None of this was possible. The dress still in hand, she spun around to look for the little door, but the door was gone. The wall plastered over. All the doors were gone.

"I need to go back," she said, but it was more to herself. "I was grown woman." She turned to Kacie, to Lizzie. "I was your mother. I was a good mother."

Kacie was still looking at her, but she was no longer smiling. "That was a long time ago, little girl. You can stay with us now."

Washing Dishes at the Lipstick Hotel

The head dishwasher smoked like a kid with a plan,
flicking ashes, picking tobacco
off his tongue, explaining
his next best job, how this
was nothing
compared to selling cars.

In the evening, after the kitchen closed,
we were left alone with supper's
stock pots and room service trays.
We played a game with coffee cups,
pictured the women   who left lipstick
on the cups.
We judged
the color, the fullness.
We took liberties,
imagined one of them the call girl
rumored on the 5th floor.

We kept the water hot, scalding, wore
rubber gloves, scrubbed fast
with nylon bristles, polished
with steel wool. With the sink empty,
we cleaned the drain trap, smacked free
the beans and pork   the gristle into the trash.
We dried,   stacked pots,
lined dishes,   tumblers,   coffee carafes.

Tomorrow needed a start fresh.
The cooks
arrived before the sun, maybe
as the call girl was closing her door.

(I owned a small motorcycle.
Home in minutes. Studied textbooks
to stay clear of Vietnam.)

The head dishwasher waited
inside the outside door
for the police to pick him up. He was
witness to something protected.

Some nights I waited with him.
He snuffed his cigarettes
in a coffee can, kept
his eye on the corner, the neon *Open*
above the bar. He never talked
about the names he could name.
I never asked. Any day, I could
drive my motorcycle
nowhere special.

Al Ortolani

Dinner at the Golden Bull

The car's headlights were like
bruised white knuckles
coming toward me after the fight.
The valet was kind, opened the door,
I stepped in and left family behind.
I didn't die
but vaporous spirits twisted in the parking lot.

We had agreed to a fresh start,
meeting at this restaurant in the canyon.
We made it through the rolls and butter,
family headstones separating me from her
across the table.
Of course, more drinks.
Of course, there were many before arrival.
Of course, prescription meds too.

My brother made a comment about Dad –
how Dad was disappointed he wasn't a jock.
That started her off.
The hope I had floated in on,
that old whoopie cushion of denial,
began to deflate like a cheap balloon.
Small mammals emerged from her clothing,
pointing with their sharp claws.
They screeched and began to gnaw
on any illusions I still had.

Across the restaurant,
Ry Cooder, a musical hero of mine,
tried to ignore us,
the loud, uncouth idiots
who commandeered the place
as he tried to finish his linguini.

Suzanne O'Connell

A Pebble for My Father

I wonder what my father's thinking
on summer movie nights at Hollywood Forever
ebullient crowds picnicking on graves
watching Tippi Hedren's supersized projection
on the icy mausoleum wall
ducking, dodging a murder of crows
while way beneath the ground
he decomposes
in that shiny, powder blue coffin we picked out for him.
Not because he fancied blue
or because he was a child, way too young to die
but because it was the cheapest one.

"Those are his orders," my uncle, a lawyer
his executor and brother had told us
as we circled the basement of the mortuary
a wallpapered, carpeted crypt.
The funeral director hesitated by each casket
listed all its features as though
we were in a fancy automobile showroom.
My father's had a bright white satin lining, a soft place
for his skeleton to reveal itself.
"How much?" the only question my uncle asked.
"He wanted you to have his money, not this place,"
he said to my brother and me.
So we settled for the blue coffin
the color of sky, the color of robin's eggs
and now the color of death.

It was closed when I saw it next
perched above the trench dug precisely for my father.
I wonder if he heard me
when I cried out from the crowd
like a scene from some melodramatic movie
"Open it."
With no benefit of formaldehyde
no mortician's makeup

no glue to keep his eyes shut
no one wanted to open it.
No one wanted me to see his face again
confirm that I would never hear his voice again
never smell his scent.

"Open it!" I called again.
Who could turn down a grieving daughter?
Who could deny this one last chance?
So they bared him to the LA November sun
his face a shocking white
that gorgeous blown-up glamour shot
of his dead girlfriend, Marge, resting on his chest.
I bent to kiss his cheek
sticky flesh
hard to peel my lips from.

They handed me the shovel, locked him away forever.
I was the first to sully that glossy
baby blue casket
with a toss of cemetery dirt.

I return there often
not for movie nights or outdoor yoga
the celebrities he slumbers with don't interest me.
I like to leave a pebble or a flower from my garden.
I like to lie myself on top of him
grass prickling my back
my head gentle on his marker
on the place that says
Beloved Father.
I like to wonder if he sees me.
I like to wonder what he's doing.

Caron Perkal

My head is a wastebasket

Although my brain retains
truckloads of knowledge,
in old age strange fragments
stick up through daily

preoccupations, plans:
bits of songs my parents
sang; songs from radio
Hit Parade they played.

Old commercial jingles.
Who would have guessed
a shampoo commercial
from 1945 would emerge.

I never know what weird
shard of pop culture
would rattle around in
my head buried perhaps

entire, ready to come
at me on sleepless nights.

Marge Piercy

What she endures

She's married to a grumpy
lump of a man. Surely, he must
have been different when they
met and fell in love.

The weakening of his body
angers him. It's someone's
fault, surely, maybe hers.
He curls around his peeves

as if he were an inchworm
clenching and unclenching
through his days. She lives
buffeted inside a storm.

Marge Piercy

They call it hampering

Stop banging on that keyboard
says Shaman the half grown kitten.
Love me, pet me, hold me. My
purr is continuous as breathing.

Am I not prettier than any poem?
Nothing on your silly computer
can love you back the way I do.
I am the cuddler staring into your

eyes, kneading your shoulder
so give up this silliness of words
and speak with your hands to me.
What you give me, I give back.

Marge Piercy

Every day a new outrage

I feel us being pushed back,
back into a time of illegal
or do it yourself abortions.

I feel us being pushed back
to gays and lesbians closeted
trans folks denied help.

I feel us being pushed back
to the hatred of Jews exploding
taken for granted in colleges.

I feel power lies in the hands
of those who despise everything
I am and ever wanted to be.

They wave their god around
like an exhibitionist's penis,
god full of angry laws.

Must I return to childhood
fears, repression an iron lid
on any spark of freedom?

Marge Piercy

Nathan Rifkin

Beach Detritus

It used to be considered a luxury to live next to the beach. Now the waters had turned toxic and every day new trash arrived on the sand. The prefabricated mansions were subject to squatters, the humble houses that had once only gone upward in value had become dirt cheap. People who lived locally were always getting sick from something, no one was sure what. Seals had been washing up dead.

David, between semesters for his last year at Cal State Dominguez Hills – and not certain he was going to make it – lumbered along next to his mother, Sarah. "This is stupid," he said. "It's cold and it's going to rain."

"This is stupid," he said again.

"It's not stupid," his mother replied. "It's important to document this. To satisfy our curiosity. And to get outside of the house."

She spent her time as a homemaker, and made it a goal to get outside every day. Without prodding, David never left home. Instead he sat at his computer all day.

At that poetry reading, he hadn't understood a word the lauded author said. It had felt good the time the professor complimented him. And, once in a while, he could hone a good sentence. But he didn't know if he had it in him anymore.

The air next to the shore smelled like rotten eggs. A dog was running just ahead of the crashing waves. Teenagers smoked pot, cranked music and necked next to cars in the parking lot. There used to be a restaurant, Rivers'End, but flooding and loss of customers had run it into the ground.

This was the way of the earth, his mother often said. Flowers wilted. Used syringes were on the ground. People rode around on bikes, scooters, mopeds, a menace to pedestrians. Vandalism on every surface: rocks, benches, signs.

It began to rain. Cold rain.

Yet it got so hot at night that the household – David, his brother John, Sarah, and Sarah's mom – could not sleep. They would gather around the television. The weather channel was of interest. It seemed like in the past year the world had changed instantly and there were storms everywhere and all the time.

Sitting on one of the jetty rocks was a girl in her early '20s photographing the panorama. Her legs swung up and down, and it looked like there was something on her head. With the sun behind her, and her hourglass figure, she looked like some kind of shadowy, retro fertility goddess. As David and his mother approached, she springboarded from the ledge.

"I've seen *you* around," she said.

David looked at his mom, slightly confused.

"Oh yeah. I walk here every day. I think it's so interesting, the stuff that washes up," said David's mom.

"I'm Eliza," the girl said. Now her beehive hair astounded David.

There was a wall of dirty sneakers piled up high and an assortment of stuffed animals leaning against a rock. There were bears, unicorns, a naked doll.

"I'm going to clean these up and give them to my godchildren. There's a group of us who try to clean the shore on Sundays. We could use a hand."

Sarah nudged David. "It might be kind of fun," she whispered.

"It starts at one if you're interested!" Eliza shouted, sounding kind of rowdy.

***

"I told her your name," Sarah said, over the cheesy scrambled eggs and toast she had made for breakfast. "Do you want another waffle, honey?"

***

"Stop puttering around the house. Why don't you go to the beach cleanup?" his mother said.

With reluctance, David walked two blocks to the beach. As he rounded the corner of the parking lot, Eliza yelled his name as if she were shouting into a void that was kind of amusing and fun.

"Dayyyyy-viiid." She approached, and added "I know, the environmentalist smokes. Incongruity," she said, taking a long drag.

She offered him a fist bump he was totally unprepared for.

"Look here," she guided him to the shore. "There's someone's mattress." She pointed to a long piece of wood with nails through it. "Bed of nails," she said.

David was following her around. Some of her friends were standing by. He found himself in a circle.

"In addition to Eliza, I'm also called Daisy," she said.

In which case, thought David, I am Dickweed.

Names were flying by faster than David could remember them.

There was a six pack, with box a few steps away, because alcohol was as popular as ever. David continued to awkwardly follow her, picking up a few things, including a broken bottle and a nerf football.

A little way down the beach, a man in a black puffer jacket and brown slacks smiled. David made out the man's churlish yet regal grin, staring down at a woman three-quarters his height.

115

"Oh my lord," Eliza snickered, pointing towards a black couple making their way across the lot. "He looks like Dennis Rodman."

"Severe dislike," said someone, looking at David, and David felt like they might be talking about him. So they were not subversives, he thought, because they were haters.

David bit his lip and fought back a war of words. These were people who drove Volvos and wore vintage t-shirts. He remembered how they looked right over him at high school functions where he unsuccessfully tried to flirt with their daughters.

"We talk a lot about beaches being public rather than privatized but we really don't want *them* here," she explained, gesturing to the black couple.

"Do you ever wish you could get rid of everyone?" Eliza asked. "Except for that girl," said Eliza, pointing out an adolescent wearing butterfly wings.

He thought about picking up trash. But he didn't feel like picking up trash. That would make him a sycophant, he thought. He felt like talking to Eliza.

David and Eliza took a break sitting on the jetty rocks. He was thinking he didn't fit in, but what if he could battle with his conscience, he could do this again – but still, Eliza was the only one in the group that accepted him.

Then she hit him with another bomb.

"I'm moving to DC," she said. "My family is, so I am."

"You know there'll be a lot of politicians there," David said, with a trace of anger but also resignation. "And people who look like Rodman."

He tried to imagine them spending a night in a sleeping bag on the sand. He was that desperate. Was it worth fighting for ideals? What about watching Netflix together? Another fantasy: a trash bonfire sendoff for Eliza.

In the waning light of what David thought of as a bland sunset, albeit red-tinged, Eliza looked inexplicably older. She was standing on the rock she stood on earlier, lighting another cigarette. She quietly nodded, scrunched up her face, and didn't say more. What happened? David thought. It was like she had been switched off.

"I've gotta go get groceries," David said. Although he was out of beer, this was pretty much a lie. "It's been nice hanging out with you," he said. "Well, see ya, Eliza."

Eliza half-smiled, and waved him away.

But before he left, David waded into the water and ignored the trash at his feet. It still smelled awful. It smelled like rotten eggs.

Two Pandemics

I remember this.
Different, but the same.
I remember young men
falling ill, and respirators,
heart monitors gone silent.
Different, but the same.
Less press back then,
not like now, when
the nightly news leads
with stories from around
the globe, provides
daily death tallies.
I don't remember
when the numbers
started to matter then.
That plague began in
a less democratic manner.
No one would even
speak its name.
Different, but the same.
Now we lean into it.
We unite to fight it,
except when we don't.
Now, like then,
the illness becomes
a political tool,
a disease weaponized.
Then, the rest of the world
only cared when they finally
understood that anyone
could get it, not just
celebrities and gay men.
I remember this, history repeating.
My heart full of loss and anger.
Everywhere a painful echo.
Different, but the same.

William Reichard

If we don't translate the forests into songs, the world will fly away

I had a vision of oblivion:

Nightdoors fell open and revealed an infinity of severed eyes. Lost boats drifted toward obliterated oceans. The trees wept into the mouth of thunder, and the wind crumbled like statues.

Our heads filled with phantoms. The world flew away on cacophonies of startled shadows.

The earth published labyrinths of tears, and the trees crumbled like the wind. The pieces of the world splayed across a sunless sky.

But oblivion had a vision:

The forests mutated into melodies, and obliterated the phantoms.

The boats bloomed into oceans. The thunder wept tears of wind and the statues became trees.

The shadows became eyes, and published a world made of infinity.

Alison Ross

Sons of Twilight

between the hours of eleven at night
and eight in the morning
i aint no poet
i am a third shift worker,
i am a nine digit punch code
i am another lost soul biding time
at a suburban grocery store
but sometimes i feel it's worth
feeling good about
the food for the neighborhood
doesn't just appear on the shelf
it's put there by the sons of twilight
the time biders the dropouts the dreamers
the hungry

Damian Rucci

Too Old for Surprises

When Mo stands up in his garden
to rest his back and knees, he can tease a forecast
out of the clouds' reticence.

Too old for surprises, Mo knows

Helen will never be herself again, their son won't call,
mass isn't about to revert to Latin,

or he himself live to harvest the beans he planted.
Mo is usually correct on most accounts.

When his hour arrives,

I hope it's like walking in on a surprise birthday party
for Mo – his entire Franco-Canadian
ancestry tooting noisemakers, wearing funny hats;

parish priest dropping by

to wish him *Felix Natalis*, and a bashful young Helen
gazing at him over her cup of punch.

Russell Rowland

Wishing You Lost

As a rule, you only walk as far into the woods
as woods let you. They have a way
of depositing you at a highway, at the backside
of a market, or where you began.

"Lost" is no easy place to reach: you must let go
of where you came from, where
you meant to get. Set course to cyclical, rather
than linear, till you don't realize

you've happened on the same boulder twice.
(It is never the same boulder twice.)
Do not let the sidereal sun deceive you – it
is not going your way.

Maybe you'll find Lost someday on your own.
It encourages humility: a place
that thrives quietly, without benefit of things
"Found" considers essential.

Love is accepted there, but not
returned. Death is merely a shadow, shifting
with the sunlight. We've yet to spoil it.
You will be welcome, if worthy.

Russell Rowland

Five-o'clock Shadow

Like mowing the lawn, shaving down to the skin
in the morning is a ritual that must be
reenacted daily to be efficacious, like sacrifice.

So falls the five-o'clock shadow upon your life.

By five at the dark of a year, the shadow discloses what
it knows: the deaths that kill you first are those

you cannot share; that hurt you most are not your own.

It tells what you won't live to see: beards seem to grow
yet a little while, postmortem, though

that is only because death contracts the skin.

It tells you of the night to come – love taking off
its beautiful disguises, to lie ashamed.

How many grow a beard to hide the face?

The hour to confess you've done what you ought not,
and not done what you ought, is five o'clock.

Russell Rowland

Stella! (Don't Ever Leave Me, Baby)

Playmate of the month the year my mother was born,
1960, Stella Stevens, only 21 and divorced,
with a five-year-old to support,
life coming at her quickly, no time to reflect –
she had to think on her feet.

Mom's life much less dramatic by contrast,
she'd always followed Stella in the movie magazines,
dreaming her starstruck dreams.
A schoolteacher, Mom met her husband in college,
U of I in Urbana, settled down in Peoria
where Dad joined his father's law firm.

Still, she had a not-so-secret passion for Stella,
who'd been born in Yazoo, Mississippi
(birth name Estelle Caro Eggleston);
Mom grew up in Indianola,
only forty miles away.

"She was a comic genius," Mom declared, defensive.
"Those *Playboy* photos? Tame by today's standards."
Bikini and side-boob shots, cleavage to excite the guys,
nothing to be ashamed about, nothing to hide.
Stella once told *The New York Times*,
"If you've got ten million people
seeing you in a layout like that,
and half of them remember the name 'Stella Stevens,'
they'll buy tickets for your movies."
Mom sure had her back.

Stella played opposite Elvis in *Girls! Girls! Girls!*,
Jerry Lewis in *The Nutty Professor,*
Played a beauty queen in *The Courtship of Eddie's Father;*
all over TV, from *Bonanza* and *The Love Boat*
to *Murder, She Wrote, Newhart* and *Night Court.*
Mom watched them all, combing *TV Guide* every week
to see if Stella was appearing on any of the shows.

It broke Mom's heart
when she learned about the Alzheimer's.
Just sixty-three when Stella died,
my mom turned into an old lady overnight,
her own life now in the rearview mirror.

Charles Rammelkamp

Oh Well, Whatever

Nevermind the owls
perched out there on dusk's glowing
horizon, or what

may or may not be
hidden behind the wizard's
gently billowing

curtains. Nevermind
the shyly inquisitive
praying mantis that

currently resides
behind your bedside lampshade
or that odd stranger

you've recently found
wading, hip-deep, with an old
kerosene lantern

through the swampy back-
woods of your dreams. And, of course
you can disregard

those leaves skittering,
scraping and rattling across
that old highway, and

the ever-shifting
nighttime geometry of
satellites, red-eye

flights and other here-
to-fore unidentified
objects routinely

crisscrossing the sky,
any given night. No, what
you need to know, right

now, is exactly
just how many fat, dirty-
faced little cherubs

with Kool-Aid smiles can
doh-see-doh on the bald head
of a bowling pin.

But, answers like that
are hard to find. Oh well, what-
ever. Nevermind.

Jason Ryberg

An Abridgement of the Light of the World

I was looking up
into the branches of
the royal star magnolia

though I don't know
what I was looking for

and I thought of Mark
up in Erie
home from work
writing his little death poems

in his own universe
but aren't we all really?

I will admit that at times
everything seems to me
all full up
with death and dying

or loss and grieving
failure and suffering

everything broken.

But then she says she has
"never been treated so well
by another person as you."

She says that, "Every day
you remind me who I am."

And that is light to go on
a full breath of clean air
something to step to.

Scott Silsbe

Against a Backdrop of Stigmas

Remember when guitarist Homeless Cody Red
met us in the Piano Van & taught me
the chords to Cameo's "Word Up"
while you waved
your hands in the air
like you don't care …
as they start to look & stare?

& there's something beautiful about singing
"We don't have the time
for psychological romance."
especially when the yearning wind is up
with the word games we played as flirty foreplay:

"You held me up" could mean "you lift me up,"
                                    "or propped me up"
"or made me an example"
                    "or you're keeping me stuck."
                              "Yikes? Am I?"
 "No, we're just playing…"
          "Or this is a stick up."
                    "Can you be stuck up & still be a suck up?"
"You make me feel sexy again."
              "Or are you using me as an excuse to feel sexy."

You were the only one who made me feel I could fit
when I was too down & out to be called eccentric.

Now the piano's like a wilting flower
trapped in the gun of a van at a junkyard

& I don't even know if you're alive …

Oh baby let's swerve

Chris Stroffolino

Doing Nothing

"Poetry might make nothing happen."
　　　　　　　– Ross Gay

After sunrise and letting the dog out,
before the day turns to business,
I sit and write a poem of this day
and wonder again what change
a poem makes. Auden said it,
"A poem changes nothing."
I've written poems for fifty years,
enough to know what not to expect,
yet on I write.

The day is clear and warm enough, so
dressed in bright jacket, helmet, and gloves,
I roll my bike out from the garage.
Embracing the autumn cool, I glide
down lanes of houses, roads of old farms,
to the worn grassy trail with its
sweet smell of trees, light flickering
through golden red leaves,
brown birds and chipmunks,
my only company. Oh, pure
circling of pedals and wheels,
thoughts vanish in this ripeness,
this steady breath of doing.
The change I'm making is
in myself – this sweet unmaking –
the nothingness of a poem.

Larry Smith

Two Tanka

My father's rough hands
spreading peanut butter
on a Golden Graham.

Yard birds calling him to work –
I sip my cup of memories.

a circle of friends
chant on hard wood floors
at the yoga studio.

out the window on a branch
a warbler echoes their song.

Larry Smith

Life is but a Dream House

at Fallingwater, Mill Run, PA

Stairs and terraces cascade down the hillside,
      eurhythmic echo of Bear Run spilling
          into Youghiogheny rapids.

I thought it would be bigger, this weekend getaway
      for a wealthy Pittsburgh family. Such is its reputation,
          luring visitors from around the world,

including a Belgian couple we make as fast friends –
      he an architect, she a photographer,
          drawn to this uniquely American mecca.

Their easy smiles and French accents bubble
      through thick summer air. We share
          their delight for Wright's clever details –

window corners without mullions, sandstone
      outcrops jutting into a living room, a canopy
          cantilevering a walkway, a swimming pool

fed by a mountain spring. The docent reminds us
      how constant water flows from the hills,
          the house prone to decay, like nations

and dreams, despite the designer's vision,
      the builder's best intentions, the owner's steadfast care.
          We move deliberately from space to space,

compressed and released, like rhododendron
      blossoms that burst open in woods around us.
          The blurred line between inside and

outside unfolds in subtle ochre and Cherokee red.
      We tour and talk, take in "The View" –
          you know the one – the house

hanging in apparent harmony with its host site.
 We snap a photo, stand in awe, content with the idea
  simply to live in the guest house, relish

light music cast by sun through single-pane windows,
 creek song tumbling through our ears.
  Ushered by a security guard, we are last to leave.

We hug one another, exchange email addresses,
 part in friendship. We exit in opposite directions.
  No one will ever build a house like this again.

Chuck Salmons

The Truth of Her

I entered the apartment, riddled with magazines and paper plates and boxes from Amazon. The dirty litter box and my mom's soiled Depends dampened the air, and I imagined microscopic fecal cells entering my nostrils.

She sat in her red leather chair, arms at her sides, head resting on her right shoulder, eyes closed, as if taking a nap.

She didn't respond when I called out, "Mom?"

I pressed on her arm, the one with the massive black bruise of unknown origin. So cold and rigid. Just like her cheek. Reminded me of a mannequin.

Still, I thought of those tiny fecal cells in my nose.

I walked away and paced the living room rug. I wondered how many fecal cells were on that rug, peppering the cat hair and the food debris. The thought distracted me from her, from the truth of her.

I went back to my mother, pressed on her again, expecting her to feel differently. The flesh was there.

Those damn fecal cells.

The truth of her was that she was dead.

Laura Shell

Terciopelo

It's true, the sky looks like a waffle
and the hills are terciopelo – velvet
or a kind of poisonous, rainforest viper.
Its other names: Bothrops asper
and Fer-de-Lance. My favorite's venom
is a hemotoxin, attacking the blood –
the worst-case scenario – but they do
eat rats that eat tree seeds, and so
are ecologically useful, Darwin's dream-girls.
Still, I would rather be
velvet, another beautiful word
that echoes its fabric – for a change,
the name and named are a good fit.
And now, the sky is stained
with dusk, pouring out beauty
like good syrup.

Patty Seyburn

18

for J

Ursa Major[1]

The late February wind grabs at our open coats
as we step through the hospital's sliding doors.
Looking up to the night sky, I pick out
the familiar stars belonging to the pair of dippers –
a habit I've had since I was a child.
I imagine my son's face, in the cusp
of manhood, haloed in a phosphorescent glow,
looking down on us from his 5th floor window.
He's watching his parents leave
because our visiting hour is over, and I wonder
if he might spot the dippers, too.

Ursa Minor[2]

18 years ago, on a bristling winter day,
I took my newborn son home from the hospital.
The orderly congratulating us as my husband
proudly transferred our slumbering bundle,
his namesake, to the Subaru's backseat.
Sliding in beside him, I was not ready
to accept our abrupt division. Tethered
to the memory of an umbilical language
that is as mysterious and familiar as the stars.

Antares[3]

48 hours ago my son left home
in a medication haze.
Telling his friends in a social media post
he was *going to a better place,*
he stopped at a convenience store,
left his phone on the counter,
then got back in his car and drove away.

Earendel[4]

As we gather in front of the convenience store's
neon 24-hour sign, I shiver in my too-thin jacket,
having thrown it on as I tripped
down the stairs to my car.
You don't think about what you're wearing
to the search party when your child
suddenly goes missing.
Stricken, glossy-eyed groups of teenagers
begin to collect in the parking lot. Some I know,
some I do not. I search the whirl of faces,
looking for some trace of my son
while a police officer writes in his notes
that he left home wearing only a tee shirt and jeans.
The winter moon does nothing to hide its indifference.

Polaris[5]

Leaving his car at a gas station,
he set out on foot like some lost Odysseus
in dirty Converse low tops.
Wandering into a nearby motel,
there's a night manager making coffee –
he's not surprised to see my son
and tells him a story about his past –
how he fled from his homeland,
leaving his family at the age of 16.
He pours the hot coffee into paper cups,
tells him *it's okay to be lost.*

Alnasl[6]

Exactly three weeks after my son's 18th birthday
a woman cries out a horrible sadness,
and I wonder if we're bad people,
me and my husband, as her sobs
quicken our graceless steps.
My husband raises his eyes to mine, and I
whisper, *it's a hospital ... things happen here,*
but we are complicit. Like a pair of thieves
fleeing their unintended crime, we don't look back.
We slink into our getaway car feeling ashamed,
feeling relieved that the strange and mutable universe
had pointed its fickle arrow at us,
and this time it had missed.

Beverly Hennessy Summa

---

[1]The Big Dipper is an asterism within the constellation Ursa Major, which is also referred to as the Wagon, the Plough, or Charles's Wain. It forms a portion of the Great Bear and can be easily spotted in the northern sky.

[2]A constellation also referred to as the asterism the Little Dipper or the Little Bear. Polaris is seen in the bowl of the Little Dipper.

[3]Also known as Alpha Scorpii, this giant red star is the brightest in the constellation Scorpius and has the nickname Scorpion's Heart. Scorpius appears as the letter J in the sky and consists of 18 named stars.

[4]The most distant star from the earth, also known as the Morning Star.

[5]Also known as the North Pole Star, Polaris is positioned at the end of the Ursa Minor's (the Little Dipper's) handle and will help with locating the Little Dipper in the sky. The North Star is also used for navigational purposes as it seems to be aligned with earth's axis or the Celestial Pole.

[6]Located in the constellation Sagittarius or the celestial Archer, this star is the arrowhead that points to Antares, the Scorpio's heart.

From the Summer of 1968

When I hand him the faded and grainy photo, my father begins
naming the faceless figures – his parents with his toddling
younger brother on the narrow deck. In the pool, like a trio of
floating heads, another brother and a sister with a neighborhood
friend and my father, preserved in eternal anticipation, one foot
on the ladder and the other at a 45-degree angle, hovering above
the water's rippled surface. You could say my father's been a
tapestry of contradiction, though two things have remained true
– his memory is as sharp as the pocketknife he's carried for as
long as I can remember, and he's always worn his Levi's, 501s
to be exact, even in the summer, except on the rare occasion
when he might swim. For this, he'd pull on a pair of cutoffs.
Back in the mid-70s, several years after the photo, and a few
years before we moved away, we'd sometimes escape our hot
city apartment and drive up county to go swimming in my
grandparents' pool. It was an above ground design, purchased
from Sears Roebuck and built by my father with his father in the
summer of 1968. They'd work all day soldering pipes and fixing
leaky sinks – it was the family business. Then, as the sun slipped
behind the suburban tree line, they'd return home, tired and
dusty, and work another hour or two on the pool. I like to
imagine it took them half the summer before they ever got a drop
of water into their father/son project – my poppy bent over with
a screwdriver in one hand, and a sweet cherry tobacco-filled pipe
in the other. He'd use my 15-year-old father for the heavy lifting.
It was the last summer they'd spend together before my father
cut out to travel to the west coast, then back east again to find
himself working at the Woodstock Festival and eventually
landing for a spell in juvenile detention. By the time he and his
family reunited, his hair had grown past his shoulders, his wrist
would don a permanent red rose, and he'd had the letters
L.O.V.E conspicuously inked across his left knuckles. Those
letters now faded like the promise of a counterculture manifesto
riding on the thin air like a hint of hash smoke. I can't be sure
what my father believed in back then, maybe not much more
than the freedom of the open road and a fresh pack of cigarettes
tucked into his shirt pocket, but soon after he met my mother, he

was plunged into fatherhood and more responsibility than I think he could get his 19-year-old head around. He sets the family photo back in the box. His eyes seem to search for a place I can't see. He smiles; tells me he's going to clear out the tangle of brushwood that has overtaken my side yard, then lights up another Pall Mall.

Beverly Hennessy Summa

'Til Just Now I Imagined 'stuck inside mobile' as in Art Work (Not Alabama).

Oh, the ragman draws circles
Up and down the block
I'd ask him what the matter was
But I know that he don't talk
And the ladies treat me kindly
And furnish me with tape
But deep inside my heart
I know I can't escape
Oh, Mama, can this really be the end ...
          – Bob Dylan
               "Stuck Inside of Mobile with the Memphis Blues Again"

It is too weird to think
we love each other so well
having attended 5th grade
through high school together

although when we knew
each other back then
not a one of us had heard
Blonde On Blonde's

double album which wasn't
written until 3 years
after Class of '63 graduated
plus had moved on.

Our parents' parents were
Old Country ragmen
and I knew one in Chicago
who sold/bought junk

maneuvering a horse-drawn
wagon, ducking down
alleyways among tin lizzies,
cold-water walkup flats.

Imagine that, all you kids
I encountered later on
in Beverly Hills mansions
included tennis courts!

But this latter-born Jew,
like Zimmerman, is
always on his lookout to
pilfer hot word bites

wherever nuggets turn up from
New York Times to
obscure *Japanese Confessions
of a Yakusa* biography

whose author is flattered by
pure plagiarism with
absolutely no intention to sue
my ignoble laureate.

Gerard Sarnat

The Christening

Pedro is on his way to his baby's baptism
after working all morning throwing mud
on cement blocks.
He gets fender-bended on Alameda
by a drunk Yaqui in a shit-colored bug with a door missing
but he doesn't have time to fuck around
and just lets it go.
When he shows up 5 minutes late to the church
the preacher slams the door in his face
and dead-bolts it.
He'd warned people not to be late
and of the fires of hell.
Pedro is locked out
and the rest of us are locked in.
Pedro's wife Yolanda is with the baby in the front row
with all the other mamas and papas and babies.
It's 108 degrees.
Preacher man won't turn the air conditioning on.
Maybe he didn't pay the bill.
Hand fans are going wild,
babies are crying,
murmurs and whispered protests fester in the pews.
Yolanda is pissed at Pedro and preacher man too.
Pedro stands outside yelling and pounding on the door,
the whole world can hear,
Pedro with hard hands and cement on his pants.
Preacher man does his thing with the babies,
mumbles the words and flicks the holy water
like you'd flick an ant
all in an orderly assembly-line manner.
Then preacher man splits out the back
through a secret exit.
A eunuch lackey unlocks the front doors
and we all flood outside
where Yolanda hands the baby to Felipe
and slaps Pedro on the left cheek hard.

Each family paid 500 dollars for the ceremony
and there are now 20 new babies
in stinky old Hermosillo
waiting to be embraced by the great unknown.

Mather Schneider

George Thomas

Shut Up

Marguerite finished the easy exercise tape and was leaving the living room when Samuel in his underwear leaped at her from the hallway. "Boo!" he said.

"Jesus, Samuel, you frightened me half to death."

He laughed and gave her a bear hug. "I love you."

Marguerite said nothing.

"Do you love me?" he said.

"I love you." She wriggled in his grip. "Let me go."

Samuel let her go. "Love you," he repeated, then he retrieved the newspaper from the porch and went to sit on the throne for as long as it took.

In the kitchen, Marguerite was making out the grocery list as he came from the throne room to lean on the counter beside her. "Those nieces of yours certainly are pooping out the babies."

Another of Marguerite's nieces was having a baby. A professional woman, Marguerite had done all she could to stimulate her nieces and nephews intellectually. She gave gifts of books to them when they were little, but none of them had finished college. She still had hopes for them. If they had their children young enough, she thought they might educate themselves later. She loved them. Having no children of her own, she imagined they might fill that need in her. They were having children of their own, now, and the emptiness of that situation bore down on her.

"I don't want to talk about it," she said.

"Honey, when I think of them and that ignorant kid, that fucking youth minister, getting hold of them and conning them away from education, I get upset. You do too. I know it."

"I don't want to talk about it," she said. "Please."

"They're happy I guess," he said.

"That's right," she said, "they are, and what else is important, so let's drop it."

"I wish I could be more like you, honey," he said.

Marguerite stuffed the grocery list in her pocketbook. "Ready?" she said.

Samuel's silence in the passenger seat felt good. Lately, he tended to run on a bit much. He could get on her nerves, but what did she expect of a man in his eighties? Mostly, she enjoyed his chatter. He entertained her, made her laugh. This morning was not one of those times. She didn't feel like grocery shopping in the first place, and she woke tired. A third hurt was her niece and the child growing inside her. She wished Sam hadn't brought it up, but he often read her moods and guessed their causes.

"Did you notice the girl on the corner back there?" he said.

"No," she said.

"I don't know any more what to make of young women."

Marguerite let him run on.

"She was with a girlfriend, probably. They were standing there, and she was shaking her booty for all to see. I don't mean swaying her hips. She was pumping her hips. Like having sex. More suggestive than tweeking," he said.

"Twerking," she told him.

"Right. Jerking your butt. Suppose a young guy, standing there next to her, gets turned on and reaches over and pinches her butt? Bam! Off to jail he goes, but she's making a clear sexual display, pumping her hips like that, isn't she?"

"I didn't see her, Sam."

"That's what I love about you, honey. You're always thinking." He reached over and stroked her leg. "Look. I understand how a woman has a right not to be touched. It's her body. I understand all that, but that girl was being totally sexual back there. Right out on the street corner. Pumping her hips. That was a sexual display like a man can see at a strip club."

"You're no prude," she said. He'd never made a secret about those places before they met. His tales about Puerto Rican prostitutes when he was in the navy interested her. His stories were part of what made him who he was.

"I want to eat lunch at Yumm! today," he told her.

The restaurant lay across Chkalov Drive from the Fred Meyer where they shopped. He enjoyed their smoky lentil soup, but Yumm! wasn't in Marguerite's plan today. She wanted to shop quickly, go home and have a peanut butter and pickle sandwich.

"Yeah," he said expansively. "Let's eat at Yumm!."

She accelerated the Civic from Mill Plain onto Chkalov through a yellow turn signal. The light changed much too quickly at that intersection.

"Wow," he said. "Great maneuver, honey."

She felt Samuel's attempt to please her. She turned into the Fred Meyer lot and parked.

"I can tell you don't want to eat at Yumm!," he said.

She revealed her pickle and peanut butter sandwich at home plan.

Samuel crossed his arms and tucked in his chin. "No Yumm!," he murmured and his lower lip began to quiver.

Her husband liked to joke about his emotions, and she didn't have to look at her spouse to know what he was up to. Most of the time, she was delighted with his hi-jinks. On other days, he could make Marguerite feel just a little guilty with his play acting, but recently he'd admitted his play acting could be about real feelings. A trait she'd long recognized.

"Stop that Sam. It's not funny."

"Sorry, honey," he said, and she heard that he meant it. "Are you sure you don't want to eat at Yumm!"

"I don't want to eat at Yumm!," she said.

"All right, no dumb Yumm! then. I'll stay mum, Mum."

He was rhyming now, word playing for laughs to get out of her doghouse. She didn't feel forgiving at the moment.

"You're really mad," he said.

She let her silence speak.

"I'm going to wait in the car," he said.

"If you want." She was not going to play guilt games with him.

Part way through her grocery list, Marguerite ran into Zelda Peterman, a high school classmate she hadn't seen for years. Twenty minutes disappeared before she noticed the time. She felt uncomfortable breaking off conversations, so it ran a bit long. Let Mr. Sammy Hammy cool his heels.

Sam wasn't in the car when Marguerite returned. She loaded the cloth bags into the trunk and closed it. He was probably on the toilet. After the bowel resection, he never knew when nature might demand his attention. He wore Depends, and there were accidents. After an accident, it took a while to get out of a diaper and clean himself up.

Marguerite started the engine, turned on the jazz station and air conditioning. She shut her lids, but she was in a hurry to get home and couldn't relax. She reopened her eyes. Several persons stood nearby on tiptoes, staring toward Chkalov Drive. Others drifted between parked cars in that direction. Then she noticed the flashing lights of an ambulance and police vehicles on Chkalov. Marguerite watched the emergency lights spin and flash hypnotically, then she began to wonder about Samuel. She climbed from the Civic and walked toward Chkalov. She found her path blocked by a crowd.

"What is it," she asked a tall man who stood next to her.

"Old man's down in the middle of the street," he said. "Looks like he got hit crossing the street."

"Oh my god," she said, and pushed at the people before her, wedging and shoving and breathless. "Get out of the way. Get out of my way. It's my husband."

People made way for her, and Marguerite quickly reached the street, but it wasn't Samuel. It was another old man, unmoving, a leg oddly bent, blood on his lips. Emergency people worked over him. He looked dead.

Struggling to catch her breath, Marguerite turned away. "It's not him," she told the nearest person.

She returned to the car, and there in the passenger seat sat Samuel.

"Where you been," he said. "Ambulance chasing?"

"Shut up," she said. "Don't say a word. We're going to Yumm! for lunch."

"Hey, you –" he began.

"Shut up," she said.

Whatever's Left of the Sun

Kid, it's like I told you
they're never gonna give you
anything back.

The days and the hours
and everything they dreamed
are lost to the ages.

And they're just gonna keep
taking and taking as if
it were their birthright

as if it were your fate
to say please and thank you

until time collapses in upon itself.

These lackeys of the dark
they are the opposite of poetry
the death of music.

Kid, you gotta take
whatever's left of the sun
wrap it in your arms
like you own the thing.

Plunge your fist into the heart of it
remember the language of fire
and sing.

William Taylor Jr.

Out on Market Street There's a Guy

Out on Market Street there's a guy
with a loudspeaker, he's talking
about my relationship
with Jesus

says my good works aren't enough
and if I really wanna get saved
I need to open my heart
and get straight with the Lord.

There's another guy with a sign
that says the government has rays
shooting down from the skies
upon me this very moment

and I can scan the code for more
information.

I guess it's good to have people
looking out for me and all
but I can't get too worked up
about any of it.

I don't think there's much I can do about the rays
and I'm concerned with more immediate things

like how Old Navy is out
of my size of the only jeans
I really like

and the place where I go to buy affordable
footwear has closed down.

If Jesus really cares about the little guy
he should think more about this kind of thing

and if he really wants to have a conversation
I'm happy to open my heart
over a handful of beers but I got
no time for his sidewalk lackeys.

See I don't need an eternity of bliss
just a good pair of skinny black jeans
so I can look good
beneath the rays.

William Taylor Jr.

Something Resembling Light

People talk big but offer
little in the way of mercy.

The lonely make me nervous
with their pleading eyes

their dreams of salvation

fumbling awkwardly about the days
waiting for something to end
or to begin.

We run out of things to say

abandon each other to various
and sundry dooms as we must.

I'm always sad when things
go away even if I never liked
them much.

I'm afraid for our failing bodies
frightened for our lonely deaths.

I imagine my sad little poems
will be forgotten sooner
rather than later

tiny sputtering flames not much use
in the face of the things
that come for us.

At best they might serve
as temporary points of grace

radiating a bit of warmth
or something resembling light

where one might pause
and rest a bit

before continuing
on whatever path
has been assigned.

William Taylor Jr.

Michael K. White

The Shroud of Turin

On his way to work on the first hot sticky day of summer, Albert noticed a tiny green bug making its way slowly across the windshield of his brand new 2020 Toyota Sphynx. He was stopped at the light at 23rd Street and was waiting impatiently for it to change. He watched as the tiny green beetle like bug traversed the open windshield at a slow steady pace. Albert waited for it to take wing and fly away. He figured as soon as the light changed it would get the hint and fly home.

He was listening to AM talk radio, the Gerry Lazo Show, a call in show about the Shroud of Turin and was it real or not. Albert has never even heard of it before, he wondered if it could really be real. It seemed like a miraculous thing to Albert, but he was skeptical because one time he had heard Gerry Lazo say there were pop bottles on the moon found by Apollo astronauts.

The light changed to green and Albert proceeded through the intersection. He kept his eyes on the bug, who had not halted its progress at all. The bug was mid windshield, right in his line of vision and didn't seem to even notice that the car was now in motion. It wasn't doing his brand new 2020 Toyota Sphynx any harm, but Albert still felt offended. He flicked his windshield wiper stalk on his steering column to flick the bug off his window and send it on its way.

Instead, the windshield wiper crushed the tiny green bug and smeared its guts in a thin fine arc of a line across his driver's side window. It didn't obstruct his vision or anything g but it was there, a reminder of a murder intentional or not. Not that it interrupted anything, but it was annoying. Albert felt a pang of guilt. He had not meant to kill only to nudge out of the way. But it was just a bug.

In fact, it wasn't a bug at all but a massive space ark full of thousands of microscopic desperate aliens from a galaxy you never heard of. After many of their years on a dying planet they had selected Earth for its abundant dirt, which they colonized. It was the answer to all their prayers and the salvation of their species or so they thought.

They were one of many millions of various alien species that regularly visited and colonized the Earth. Most of these aliens were tiny, so tiny that the inhabitants of Earth did not notice them or thought, like Albert did, that they were just bugs. Thus, countless attempts to tame the savage Earth had been squashed on the bottoms of many shoes and devoured by numerous cats.

In their world, they were giants, but here on Earth their colossal transports, the height of their technology, resembled little green bugs. The conglomeration of body and mechanical fluids that smeared the fine line on Albert's windshield was the point where their ancient and formidable civilization was forever snuffed out.

Albert went on through his day not even thinking about the death of thousands that he had caused by an innocent flick of his windshield wiper stalk. He was even yawning when he did it. But the smeared line bothered him. It tugged at him. He hadn't meant to kill the bug. It was just a bug. On the way home from work Albert decided it would be a good idea to wash his car. To get the bug guts off his window and his conscience.

He pulled into a bay at Sudsy's car wash and filled the box with quarters until a high-pressure spray came sputtering then booming out. Albert made sure to wash his windshield extra good because he knew from past experience how hard it could be to get bug guts off a windshield. And wouldn't you know when he drove off, he could still see the thin fine arc of a line left by the wiper's stroke.

Later at home, he took some paper towels and Windex into the garage where his wife was replanting tomato plants from egg cartons to pots. She didn't look up or ask him what he was doing. Albert squirted some Windex and rubbed it vigorously with the paper towel. After a few more squirts, he could no longer see the line.

"Have you ever heard of the Shroud of Turin?" he asked his wife.

Ali Shehzad Zaidi

Confinement as Liberation

Beginning in 1951, the Urdu poet Faiz Ahmed Faiz spent four years in solitary confinement for his involvement in the Rawalpindi Conspiracy Case. Imprisonment was the seminal experience that ignited his creativity and shaped his poetry. In a letter to his wife Alys, dated June 24, 1951, Faiz wrote, "I have just finished my sixth poem after being arrested. That means that have I written twice as much in the past three months as I had written in the previous three years" ("Faiz to Alys" 119). Having been liberated from the mundane happenstance of the everyday, Faiz had discovered the magical present to which the mystics beckon.

In another letter to Alys, dated November 9, 1951, Faiz described the fresh perspective that imprisonment had given him:

> The prison is a world in itself, quite separate from the rest of the world. One can even say that it is a kind of an "afterworld," so remote it is from the ordinary world. From its towering heights one can cast a comprehensive look on the human world below – that is if one wants to. As for me, I often don't even look that way. Every moment of solitude has plenty of attractions of its own to keep my heart beguiled. ("Faiz to Alys" 124)

In 1958, General Ayub Khan seized power in a coup and the military regime took over *The Pakistan Times*, the progressive newspaper of which Faiz had been chief editor since Pakistan's independence in 1947. That year, Faiz was again detained under the Pakistan Security Act and spent a year in solitary imprisonment. Ironically, the restrictions on Faiz's movement spread his verses far and wide. His lyrics were featured in many films and millions learned them by heart throughout the Indian subcontinent.

In an essay, Faiz explained how physical confinement had heightened his senses, integrating them into poetry of pain and longing:

> In prison, particularly in prison par excellence which I have experienced twice, namely, solitary confinement, the mind has nothing to feed on except its sensory impressions and its pain. The minutiae of external phenomena are matched by the sharply etched detail of their reflection in the mind. This process together with the emotive element facilitates the transliteration of the visual into the verbal. ("Impact" 21-22)

Besides its sensual quality, Faiz's revolutionary poetry possesses a powerful spiritual depth, as in "Dawn of Golden Eagles" with its evocative prison imagery:

Awake –
my shackled rivers –
bring death to your tormentors.
Cracks appear in the leaden sky.
Fortresses crumble
and dungeons are on fire.
The hour is fast approaching
when crowns will be tossed
on sandy beaches
and thrones kicked into the sea
from the tallest cliffs.

The poem's title recalls the Buddhist and Orthodox Christian iconography in which gold represents divine light. The eagle, which represents nobility and spiritual ascension, is enveloped in golden light. The dungeons on fire evoke the melting of the "mind forg'd manacles" that William Blake decries in his poem "London" (393).

This divine sensibility awakens, in the words of Faiz, a beauty that "is as tangible as reality and as elusive as ghost ... ecstasy, torment, experience and memory all rolled into an 'infinite variety'" ("Concept" 128) that unifies the spiritual and the sensual. In every endeavor, whether as a journalist, editor, or educator, Faiz sought to promote artistic expression, and the apprehension of beauty, in film, painting, poetry, and dance. However, these cultural forms began to wither under the repression of successive military regimes, culminating in that of General Zia-ul-Haq which lasted from 1977 to 1988.

Financed by the United States and Saudi Arabia, Zia sponsored terror groups to overthrow the socialist government of Afghanistan and to repress opposition within Pakistan. Zia mandated that Pakistani Muslims pay their religious charitable contribution, known as *zakat,* to the government. The military regime then diverted much of the funds, ostensibly for the needy, to religious schools where famished children were imparted a cruel creed.

With the press heavily censored and opposition parties banned, Faiz's poetry resonated among students, workers, and the poor. Faiz left Pakistan in 1979, shortly after Zia had former Prime Minister Zulfiqar Ali Bhutto hanged after a sham trial. In a 1981 interview, Faiz explained that his exile, unlike those of the Turkish poet Nazim Hikmet and the Palestinan poet Mahmoud Darvesh had been voluntary:

I was not ordered to leave. I saw that things were not quite right, so I thought I would take a holiday from the situation. But my situation is different from that of Hikmat and Dervesh. I am not deprived in the sense in which they are. I can always go home. No one has stopped me. I have the choice ... However, the anguish of separation from one's loved ones is not lessened by this awareness. ("Interview" 31)

Faiz returned to Pakistan a year before his death in 1984. Many thousands thronged his mile-long funeral procession in Lahore. By then, Pakistan was undergoing a process of cultural and linguistic debasement. In Orwellian fashion, words and phrases of Persian origin began to vanish from everyday Urdu-language usage. Pakistanis began to use an awkward hybrid construction, *Allah hafiz*, instead of the Urdu expression *khuda hafiz* that means "May God protect you" or "God be with you" (the English word "goodbye" is itself a contraction of "God be with ye").

Wahabi, Deobandi, and Salafi clerics deem the word *khuda* unIslamic because the word predates Islam and supposedly refers to some other god other than the one that they worship, or pretend to worship. However, Muslim and Christian Arabs alike use the word *Allah* for God. The phrase *Allah hafiz* is a strange admixture of Arabic and Urdu that no one utters save Pakistanis who take linguistic cues from benighted clerics and military dictators.

Some rather doctrinaire Pakistanis even insist on using the Arabic word for Islamic prayer, *salah,* instead of the Urdu word *namaz* which is used in Turkic and Persianate languages throughout western Asia. Faiz, who held masters degrees in Arabic and English, was also fluent in Persian and French. His poetry embodies the rich confluence of languages that gave rise to Urdu. Notwithstanding, the lexical impoverishment of Urdu continues apace in a country whose national anthem consists almost entirely of Persian words that are cognate with Urdu.

In "No Messiah for Broken Glass," Faiz rues the mean-spirited and intolerant ethos that has befallen Pakistan:

Pearl, ruby, sapphire –
crystal decanter, tulip glass.
Whatever breaks
is forever annulled.
Your tears will not mend it.
No use waiting –
hoping – waiting.
There is no messiah for broken glass.

The moon is wrecked
with dry-rot.
What talisman now
to exorcise your fears?
Green water
on blades of grass.
City of thieves.
Old avenues. Walnut-shells.
Faded curtains.
What we remember
is always ours.
Strange mirror –
It does not reflect colours –
only black and white.

The decanter and glass, which hold the wine of love, are irremediably broken. So too are the legendary gems that enable us to see in the night, which are referenced in Persian epic poems about the legendary Alexander the Great. Those rare jewels of inestimable value are holy mirrors that reveal the divine soul within us. The moon, that emblem of human aspiration and longing, is another such mirror, but in this poem the moon has lost its potency.

The green water on grass appears as a new talisman of revival and regeneration. The city of thieves recalls the kleptocracy into which Pakistan has devolved. In this regard, the faded curtains evoke the interminable cultural and religious confinement of Pakistanis. The walnut leaves, used to induce abortion, hint at their stillborn dreams and aspirations, as well as the loveless marriage between the people and their rulers. In this poem, remembrance leads to healing and recovery. The strange mirror that reflects only black and white conveys a sense of a polarized society as well as of lives devoid of joy and color.

As the most celebrated and widely translated Urdu poet of the twentieth century, Faiz became a cultural ambassador who restored Pakistan to the world. He wrote travelogues about his trips to Cuba and the Soviet Union and became friends with such writers as Pablo Neruda and Yevgeny Yevtushenko. Like Nelson Mandela, Faiz discovered that confinement only amplified his voice and extended its reach. Faiz knew that his verses would endure, as he conveys in "The Day Death Comes":

How will death come?
Like the first kiss –
spontaneous, burning nectar –
roses on a Caucasian plateau

and the moon's torment.

Early in the morning
or late at night –
an icy torrent of stars
cascading down a cobbled street.
Mysteriously the doors open.

Like the raw end of a nerve.
Shadow of the hangman's rope.
Dark clouds rubbing their bellies
on my rooftop. The stench of wolves.
But on scarlet-sweet lips, my name – my name.

Death arrives like the first kiss to return us to the Beloved. Doors open
to reintegrate us into the cosmos. The roses on a Caucausian plateau
recall the dawn of cultural memory when the Caucasus sustained ancient
civilizations. The wolves and the hangman's rope evoke the danger that
pursued Faiz throughout his life. This vulnerability became his strength,
namely, a legacy of love as suggested by the image of "scarlet-sweet
lips." Scarlet is the color of blood and wounds have the shape of lips. At
the same time, the image also confirms that Faiz's poems, dyed in the
color of love, overcame the oblivion into which his enemies sought to
cast him.

Works Cited

Blake, William. "London." *Literature: Craft and Voice. Volume 2: Poetry*. Ed. Nicolas
Delbanco and Alan Cheuse. New York: Mcgraw-Hill, 2010: 393.

Faiz, Faiz Ahmed. "The Concept of Beauty," In *Culture and Identity*. Ed. Sheema
Majeed. Oxford University Press, Karachi, 2005: 127-128.

Faiz, Alys and Faiz Ahmed Faiz. "Faiz to Alys to Faiz: Some Prison Letters." *Annual
of Urdu Studies* 5 (1985): 117-124.

Faiz, Faiz Ahmed. "Impact of Prison Life on Imagery," In *Culture and Identity*. Ed.
Sheema Majeed. Oxford University Press, Karachi, 2005: 21-22.

Faiz, Faiz Ahmed. Interview by Muzaffar Iqbal. *Indian Writers at Work*. Ed. Devindra
Kohli. B. R. Publishing, Delhi, 1991: 21-36.

John Brantingham

Thaddeus Rutkowski's *Safe Colors*

Thaddeus Rutkowski calls his newest book, *Safe Colors,* "a novel in short fictions." It is part of a new trend in fiction, the novel-in-flash and the novella-in-flash. While this is not a completely new genre, the practitioners of it often use it to create a new kind of realism in fiction. In longer works of fiction, writers are often required to skip over the small events of people's lives because they do not have relevance to a larger story. What the writers of flash fiction often understand is that those events, moments that do not necessarily relate to a story arc, often constitute the most meaningful parts of our lives. As these writers expand into novels-in-flash and novellas-in-flash, they are able to capture lives closer to the ways that we experience them, with small events without clear story arcs, forming our personalities, fears, and joys. *Safe Colors* does this exceptionally well, and Rutkowski's novel gives us a look at what it means to be human. A book like this reminds me that we create meaning out of a series of events and this meaning is what I refer to as life. It is a brilliant book, the kind that helps one develop a greater compassion for those around us. It reminds us that we are not the only people on earth experiencing our share of pain, but that we all live these kinds of lives.

The first section of *Safe Colors* follows the youth of the main character as he tries to understand the world and his place in it. Like so many people, he feels like an outsider. And in fact, he is treated like one as the son of a mixed-race couple, whose father's addictions keep him from being fully present in his family's life. The emotion of this time is captured well in the story "Nowhere Boy":

> That would have helped, if some actor showed up where I lived or where I went to school. That would have proved I was Someone. But I knew no TV actors. I was No One.
> I didn't have high expectations for a change in my situation. I just wanted to get to school on time (4).

Like so many people, he feels stuck and outside and not a part of the passionate kind of life he wants. Instead, his problems seem so banal, and this idea creates a frustration inside of him. His father wants to make it as a painter, but doesn't, so the family must live on the small wages his mother brings in. In school, his outsider status is confirmed and reconfirmed even in the school play where he and his siblings "didn't win major roles, but we were selected to play island dancers" (15).

And so his life proceeds. There are no moments of high drama as television or the movies might portray it, but there is the endless, painful wearing down that people experience as a result of the intolerance and day-to-day injustice of other people. As such, it is far more realistic than so much of the fiction I read. There is no one event that creates an easily definable meaning, but just the constant difficulty of life that we make for each other and people of color experience so much more frequently and painfully. It is not the big event. It's the ruthlessness of the everyday moments.

So much of the last sections is about the sacrifices we make as adults and the losses we all experience as we age. By this time, the main character has found his place in the world and understands how to deal with it. It is then that he starts to experience the kinds of losses that people experience as they age. Once again, these moments are not necessarily large and dramatic, but that does not make them less profound. In fact for me, these are much more profound because I am able to relate them to my life. The sacrifices he makes are for his wife and daughter. Unlike his father, he does so consistently and without complaint. He works at a job that he dislikes. When he discusses it after he is eventually fired, he talks to a therapist about not what made it interesting but how he was able to bear it:

> 'You didn't seem to like your job very much,' she said, 'but you didn't do anything about it.'
> 'I did a lot,' I said. 'I had a double life.'
> 'You should celebrate that,' she said, 'You should be happy about all the things you did in secret. You should be glad no one found out' (231).

The victory here is not in finding great joy, but finding ways to make slogging through the bitterness of life bearable. His losses too stack up as people around him and in his family die, and there is no great lesson in their deaths or in their lives, not one that can be summed up in a pithy statement because our lives are far more complex than that. The main character is just trying to live with that complexity as we all do. In the final story, he thinks about his father and brother, both dead now. "My father and brother were always at each other's throats, but now they shared a stone" (266). It is as though the many meanings of who we are is in that statement. Yes, the father and son had conflict, but there was connection too. Neither the bond nor the strife defines them. Nothing does define a person or people's relationship fully, and Rutkowski demonstrates this fact so well.

I do not know to what degree the main character of *Safe Colors* is based on the author, but the life Rutkowski creates through him is hyper-realistic. It feels real because it feels like the way I have experienced my life. The memories I have keep coming back to certain themes and ideas without creating a narrative of any kind. So do his. Instead, they are events that help us and him to understand where he has been and what has led him to this place in his life. In this, it accomplishes what a great novel-in-flash can.

✥ Some Particulars ✥

JC Alfier's most recent book is *The Shadow Field* (Louisiana Literature, 2020). Journal credits include *The Emerson Review, Faultline, New York Quarterly, Notre Dame Review, Penn Review, Southern Poetry Review,* and *Vassar Review.* He is also an artist doing collage and double-exposure work.

Jen Ashburn is author of *The Light on the Wall* (Main Street Rag, 2016) and has published in numerous venues, *The Fiddlehead, The Writer's Almanac* and *New Ohio Review.* She holds an MFA from Chatham U and lives in Pittsburgh.

Mary Isabel Azrael co-edits *Passager* books and journal featuring writers over 50. She leads poetry workshops, most recently at Johns Hopkins. She wrote the libretto for *Lost Childhood,* an opera performed in Tel Aviv, New York, Washington, and Los Angeles. A recent exhibition, Parallel Play, combined her poems with visual images by John P. Wise. She has four poetry collections and poems in *Prairie Schooner, Harpers, Calyx* and elsewhere.

A.R. Bender is a writer of German and Native heritage now living in Tacoma, Washington, USA. His multi-genre short stories, flash fiction, and poetry have been published in numerous literary journals, most recently in: *Guilty Crime Magazine, Hidden Peak Press, Bristol Noir, Pulp Modern, Close To the Bone, Thriller Magazine,* Sein Und Werden, *Mystery Tribune.*

Ace Boggess is author of six books of poetry, most recently *Escape Envy.* His writing has appeared in *Indiana Review, Michigan Quarterly Review, Notre Dame Review, Harvard Review,* and other journals. An ex-con, he lives in Charleston, WV, where he writes and tries to stay out of trouble. His seventh collection, *Tell Us How to Live,* is forthcoming (Fernwood, 2024).

McKenzie Bonar is a student at the U of Pittsburgh-Greensburg, majoring in Education and Creative Writing. Her poems were recently published in *Trailer Park Quarterly.* She waits tables and teaches eighth grade in Latrobe, PA.

Caleb Bouchard is author of *The Satirist: Prose Poems* (Suburban Drunk). His next book, *79 Nonets,* will be released in 2024. He lives outside Atlanta, GA, where he teaches college-level writing. Find him on Instagram @calebbouchard.

Amanda J. Bradley has published three poetry collections with NYQ Books: *Queen Kong, Oz at Night,* and *Hints and Allegations,* and has published fiction, essays, and poems widely in anthologies and literary magazines such as *Paterson Literary Review, Griffel, Lips, Rattle, New York Quarterly, Kin, The Nervous Breakdown, Apricity Magazine,* and *Gargoyle.* Amanda is a graduate of the MFA program at The New School, and holds a PhD in English and American Literature from Washington U in St. Louis. She lives in Indianapolis, and her website can be found at www.amandajbradley.com.

Caleb Coy is a freelance editor with a Masters in English from Virginia Tech. He lives with his family in southwest Virginia. His work has appeared in *Potomac Review, Flyway, The Common, The Fourth River*, and *Harpur Palate*. In 2015 he published his debut novel, *An Authentic Derivative*.

Carl Miller Daniels is 71 years old. He says that like it's some kind of accomplishment. Maybe it is. His X-rated *Tumblr* blog is gone. His X-rated new *Tumblr* blog is gone. His X-rated *BlogSpot* blog remains: carlmillerdaniels.-blogspot.com/.

Holly Day works as an instructor at The Richard Hugo Center in Seattle and at the Loft Literary Center in Minneapolis.

Lenny DellaRocca is founder and co-publisher of *South Florida Poetry Journal – SoFloPoJo*. His work has appeared in many lit-mags since 1980, *Chiron Review* among them. *Festival of Dangerous Ideas* is his second full-length collection of poetry. He has two chapbooks.

David Denny's most recent books are *Angel of the Waters* and *Sometimes Only the Sad Songs Will Do* (Shanti Arts). His work has appeared in *The Sun, Narrative, Catamaran, Rattle*, and *Chiron Review*. A former student of the late great Gerry Locklin, he lives in California with his wife Jill and their Belgian Shepherd Ginny. More info: daviddenny.net.

Faiz Ahmad Faiz (1912-1984) was one of the most exemplary poets of the Indian subcontinent. His poetic voice, full of revolutionary fervor and also revolutionary melancholy, tugged at the heart of the Urdu reader particularly because he filled his poetry with words used mostly in pre-modern ghazals which have a resonance of their own. Faiz was able to convey the message of revolution without compromising the delicate subtlety of Urdu literary vocabulary. He published eight volumes of poetry in his lifetime.

Lyn Fenwick is an award-winning author who writes poetry for her own pleasure but enjoys the work of others.

Michael Flanagan was born in the Bronx, NY and lives on Prince Edward Island, Canada. His full length collection, *Days Like These* (Luchador) is out now. His chapbook, *A Million Years Gone*, is available from *Nerve Cowboy*'s Liquid Paper Press.

Tony Gloeggler is a lifelong resident of NYC and his work has recently appeared in *Paterson Literary Review, Columbia Poetry Review, Rattle, Nerve Cowboy*, and *Trajectory*. His collections include *One Wish Left* (Pavement Saw) and *The Last Lie* (NYQ). *Until the Last Light Leaves* is forthcoming from NYQ Books.

Jay Griswold graduated Colorado State U in 1979 with a masters degree in creative writing. He worked for many years as a ranger for the Colorado

Division of parks, primarily on the water patrol. His books are *Meditations for the Year of the Horse* (Leaping Mountain, 1986), *The Landscape of Exile* (West End, 1993), and *Conquistador* (Main Street Rag, 2005).

Eric Grow lives in Manhattan Beach, CA with his wife, two children and three cats. He has been published previously in *The Wormwood Review* and *The Peters Black and Bluer Guide to Current Literary Journals*.

Lisa M. Hase-Jackson is author of *Insomnia in Another Town* (Clemson U, forthcoming), and *Flint and Fire* (The Word Works, 2019). She is a Pushcart-nominate poet whose work can be found in *Limp Wrist, Tipton Poetry Journal, Cimarron Review*, and *South Carolina Review.* She teaches English and creative writing at Trident Community College in Charleston, SC.

Alicia Hilton is an author, editor, arbitrator, professor, and former FBI Special Agent. Her work has appeared in *Breakwater Review, Creepy Podcast, Eastern Iowa Review, Litro, Modern Haiku, Mslexia, Neon, Stoneboat Literary Journal, Vastarien, World Haiku Review, Year's Best Hardcore Horror Volumes 4, 5 & 6*, and elsewhere. Her website is https://aliciahilton.com. Follow her on Twitter @aliciahilton01 and Bluesky @aliciahilton.bsky.social.

Kylie A Hough writes on unceded Yugambeh Country. A finalist and recipient of various writing awards, Kylie is a 2024 Best of the Net nominee, 2024 NWF/joanne burns Microlit Award finalist, 2023 Pushcart Prize nominee, 2022 Woollahra Digital Literary Award finalist, and a 2021 CA/ASA Award Mentee. Her poetry, essays and short stories are published locally and internationally.

Victor D. Infante is features editor for *The Worcester Telegram & Gazette* and editor for *Worcester Magazine*. He has appeared in dozens of journals, including *The Collagist, Barrelhouse, Pearl, Spillway* and *The Banyan Review*, as well as in anthologies such as *Poetry Slam: The Competitive Art of Performance Poetry, Spoken Word Revolution Redux, The Last American Valentine: Poems to Seduce and Destroy, Aim For the Head: An Anthology of Zombie Poetry, The Incredible Sestina Anthology* and all three *Murder Ink: Tales of New England Newsroom Crime* anthologies. He lives in Worcester, MA, with his wife, the poet Lea C. Deschenes, and their army of ferrets.

Akiva Israel is a prison poet and an artist doing time in a prison for men. Currently she's working on her short fiction piece, "A Strange Little Girl," about Peter Pan's twin sister, Penelope Pan. In 2023, guards in California Men's Colony mutilated and destroyed thousands of pages and pieces of her visual-poetic art. She recently settled her case, Israel v. Gibbs, for monetary damages, yet staff continue to desecrate her First Amendment rights.

Lori Jakiela is author of seven books, most recently *They Write Your Name on a Grain of Rice: On Cancer, Love and Living Even So* (Atticus, 2023). She lives in Trafford, PA. Her website is http://lorijakiela.net.

Sarah Mackey Kirby grew up among magnolia trees and lightning bugs in Louisville, KY. She is author of *The Taste of Your Music* (Impspired, 2021). Her poems appear in *ONE ART, Ploughshares, Third Wednesday*, and elsewhere. She and her husband divide their time between Louisville and Dayton, OH.

Craig Kirchner is retired and thinks of poetry as hobo art. He loves storytelling and the aesthetics of the paper and pen. He has had two poems nominated for the Pushcart, and has a book of poetry, *Roomful of Navels*. After a writing hiatus he has recently been published in several dozen journals.

Zack Kopp holds an MFA in Writing from Vermont College of Fine Arts. You can find his blog at www.campelasticity.com and all his books at Amazon. His latest, *Uneasy World*, is a look at the metaphysics of AI (artificial intelligence) and human creativity including a conversation about Edgar Cayce and UFOs with Jami Cassady. He lives currently in Denver, CO.

Michael Lauchlan has contributed to many publications, including *New England Review, Virginia Quarterly Review, The North American Review, Louisville Review, Poet Lore*, and *Lake Effect*. His most recent collection is *Trumbull Ave.* (WSU Press).

Scott Laudati runs *Bone Machine* from an apartment in NYC with his iguana, Donna. He is the author of *Play The Devil and Camp Winapooka*. Visit him anywhere @ScottLaudati.

Kevin D. LeMaster is author of the chapbook *Mercy* (Arroyo Seco, 2023). His poems have been found at *SheilaNaGig* online, *Gyroscope Review, Hive Avenue Literary Journal, Main Street Rag, Barely South Review, Mantis, Amistad* and others.

Paul Luikart is the author of the short story collections *Animal Heart* (Hyperborea, 2016), *Brief Instructions* (Ghostbird, 2017), *Metropolia* (Ghostbird, 2021) and *The Museum of Heartache* (Pski's Porch, 2021.) He serves as an adjunct professor of fiction writing at Covenant College in Lookout Mountain, GA. He and his family live in Chattanooga, TN.

Sean Padraic McCarthy has stories forthcoming in *Epoch, South Carolina Review*, and *Louisiana Literature*, and is currently at work upon a new novel.

Joshua McGuire is an award-winning opera librettist. Current projects include a multimedia opera on Hesse's *Siddhartha* with composer Murray Hidary, as well as an opera with Evan Mack on pioneering AIDS activist Ruth Coker Burks. The recipient of fellowships from Opera America, Washington National Opera, and Yaddo, McGuire currently teaches at Vanderbilt University's Blair School of Music. www.joshuamcguire.com.

Tamara Madison is author of *The Belly Remembers*, *Wild Domestic* and *Moraine*, all published by Pearl Editions. Her work has appeared in *Your Daily Poem*, *A Year of Being Here*, *Nerve Cowboy*, *Writer's Almanac* and others. She is thrilled to have recently retired from teaching English and French in an LA high school.

Giovanni Mangiante is a bilingual poet from Lima, Peru. His work appears in *Book of Matches*, *Open Minds Quarterly*, *Studi Irlandesi*, *Three Rooms Press*, and more. His bilingual collection *Poems Written Under Peruvian Winters* was published by Book Hub Publishing Group. He lives with his dog, Lucy.

Michael Montlack is author of two poetry collections, most recently *Daddy* (NYQ Books), and editor of the Lambda Finalist essay anthology *My Diva: 65 Gay Men on the Women Who Inspire Them* (U of WI). His poems recently appeared in *Poetry Daily*, *Prairie Schooner*, *North American Review*, *december*, *Cincinnati Review*, and *phoebe*. His prose has appeared in *The Rumpus*, *Huffington Post* and *Advocate.com*. In 2022 his poem won the Saints & Sinners Poetry Award (for LGBTQ writers). He lives in NYC, where he teaches Poetry at CUNY City College.

Michael Miller lives in Amherst, MA. His poems have appeared in *Sewanee Review*, *Kenyon Review*, *Raritan*, and *Yale Review*. His third book, *Darkening the Grass*, was a "Must Read 2013" selection of the Massachusetts Book Awards.

Lisa Marguerite Mora's writing has been published widely including in *Rattle* and *Galway Review*. Semifinalist *Tom Howard Poetry Contest*; her micro fiction is forthcoming in *Once Upon A Time – A Magical Storybook* by Lori Preusch (Dandelion Press.) Lisa has recently completed a first novel. Literary services offered: https://www.lisamargueritemora.com.

Suzanne O'Connell is a poet living in Los Angeles. Her recently published work can be found in *Drunk Monkeys*, *Wrath Bearing Tree*, *Paterson Literary Review*, *North American Review*, *Poet Lore*, and *Summerset Review*. Her two poetry collections, *A Prayer for Torn Stockings* and *What Luck*, were published by Garden Oak Press.

Al Ortolani's poetry has appeared in journals such as *Rattle*, *New York Quarterly*, and *Prairie Schooner*. His most recent poetry collection is *The Taco Boat* (New York Quarterly, 2022). His first novel, *Bull in the Ring*, was just released by Meadowlark Books in Emporia, KS. He lives in the Kansas City area.

Caron Perkal lives in Southern California.

Marge Piercy has published 19 poetry collections, including *On the Way Out, Turn Off the Lights* and *Made in Detroit* [Knopf]; 17 novels including *Sex Wars*. PM Press reissued *Vida, Dance the Eagle to Sleep*; they brought out short stories *The Cost of Lunch, Etc* and *My Body, My Life* [essays, poems]. She has read at more than 500 venues here and abroad.

Charles Rammelkamp is Prose Editor for BrickHouse Books. His poetry collection, *A Magician Among the Spirits,* was a 2022 Blue Light Press Poetry winner. In 2023 he published *Transcendence* (BlazeVOX), a collection of flash, *Presto* (Bamboo Dart), *See What I Mean?* (poems and flash, Kelsay).

William Reichard is a writer, editor, and educator. His eighth collection of poetry, *In the Evening*, will be published by Broadstone Books in 2024.

Nathan Rifkin is a senior at Sonoma State University working toward a collection of short stories for his capstone project. This would be his first published story. Shout-out to his mom.

Alison Ross, *Clockwise Cat* publisher and editor, pioneered the genre of Zen-Surrealism and the tenets of Zen-Surrealist Socialism, and uses those as her guiding aesthetic. Alison believes that poetic intuition knifes through the murk of the mundane and mutates mediocrity into a Utopia of the Dynamic. Alison writes reviews and editorials in various publications, including *PopMatters*.

Russell Rowland writes from New Hampshire's Lakes Region, where he has judged high-school poetry, Out Loud competitions. His work appears in *Except for Love: New England Poets Inspired by Donald Hall* (Encircle), and *Covid Spring, Vol. 2* (Hobblebush). His latest poetry book is *Magnificat* (Encircle).

Damian Rucci is a touring poet from New Jersey and author of nine books of poetry. He is founder of the NJ Poetry Renaissance and focus of the PBS documentary *Voices in The Garden*. A twice resident of the Osage Arts Community in Missouri, Damian has spent the last 10 years bouncing around the country performing in universities, bookstores, dive bars, basements, and tattoo parlors. He is the host of ten poetry series including Puff Puff Poems and Poems & Punchlines.

Jason Ryberg is author of 18 books of poetry, six screenplays, a few short stories. He is an artist-in-residence at The Prospero Institute of Disquieted P/o/e/t/i/c/s and Osage Arts Community. He is an editor and designer at Spartan Books. His latest collection of poems is *Fence Post Blues* (River Dog, 2023). He lives part-time in Kansas City, MO with a rooster named Little Red and a Billy-goat named Giuseppe, and part-time somewhere in the Ozarks, near the Gasconade River, where there are also many strange and wonderful woodland critters.

Chuck Salmons has served as part of the Ohio Poetry Association leadership team for more than a decade. His poems have appeared in numerous journals, including *Pudding Magazine, Evening Street Review, The Ekphrastic Review*, and *Sheila-Na-Gig Online*. He received a 2018 Ohio Arts Council Individual

Excellence Award for poetry and has published two chapbooks, *Stargazer Suite* and *Patch Job*. chucksalmons.com.

Gerard Sarnat, MD has authored four collections, is widely published including recently by Dartmouth, Penn, Oberlin, Brown, Harvard, Stanford, Columbia, Chicago, Wesleyan, Johns Hopkins, *Review Berlin, New Ulster, Gargoyle, Margie, Main Street Rag, New Delta Review, Free State Review, Brooklyn Review, Los Angeles Review, San Francisco Magazine, New York Times.*

Mather Schneider's poetry and prose have been published in many places since 1995. His first novel, *The Bacanora Notebooks*, was recently released by Anxiety Press. He lives in Tucson and works as an exterminator.

Patty Seyburn has published five books of poems: *Threshold Delivery* (Finishing Line, 2019); *Perfecta* (What Books, Glass Table Collective, 2014); *Hilarity* (New Issues, 2009), *Mechanical Cluster* (Ohio State U, 2002) and *Diasporadic* (Helicon Nine, 1998). With my last 12 words, I would like to acknowledge my use of three exclamations points in one poem.

Laura Shell lives in South Carolina with her husband of 35 years and her dog, Groot. One of her works of fiction was featured in an online publication in April of 2024.

Scott Silsbe was born in Detroit. He now lives in Wilkinsburg, PA. His poems and prose have appeared in numerous periodicals and have been collected in four books: *Unattended Fire, The River Underneath the City, Muskrat Friday Dinner*, and *Meet Me Where We Survive*. He is also an editor at Low Ghost Press.

Larry Smith is a poet, fiction writer, literary biographer of Kenneth Patchen and Lawrence Ferlinghetti, as well as editor and publisher of Bottom Dog Press in Huron, OH since 1985. A native of the industrial Ohio Valley, he now lives with his wife Ann along the shores of Lake Erie. His most recent publications include *The Thick of Thin: Memoirs, The Pears: Poems, Mingo Town and Memories*, and *Connections: Tanka by Larry Smith and Haiku by Barbara Sabol.*

Chris Stroffolino is teaching at Laney College, and being priced out of Oakland. He recently published a memoir with Dave Roskos' Vendetta Books, and a book of poems, *Drinking from What I Once Wore* (Crisis Chronicles, 2018). You may listen, and download, some of his music for free [don't pay, please!] at: soundcloud.com/chrisstroffolino/sets/audition-4-a-practice-people.

Beverly Hennessy Summa's poems have appeared in *Trailer Park Quarterly, Nerve Cowboy,* and *Plum Tree Tavern*. She has a BA in English. Beverly owns a music school and store with her husband and lives in South Salem, NY with her family.

William Taylor Jr. lives and writes in San Francisco. He is author of numerous books of poetry, and a volume of fiction. His work has been published widely in literary journals, including *Rattle* and *New York Quarterly*. He was a recipient of the 2013 Kathy Acker Award, and edited *Cocky Moon: Selected Poems of Jack Micheline* (Zeitgeist, 2014). His latest poetry collection, *A is Room Above a Convenience Store* (Roadside Press).

George Thomas, a Navy veteran and CNC machinist, earned his MFA at Eastern Washington U. He co-founded the literary magazine *Willow Springs* there and, later, published and edited his own monthly *George & Mertie's Place* for six years. His work has appeared in magazine like *Anglo-Welsh Review, Work Literary Magazine, Willow Springs, Bellowing Ark, Crab Creek Review, Kestrel, Illuminations* and *North Dakota Quarterly*.

Michael K. White wasted his youth as a member of the semi-legendary New York playwriting group Broken Gopher Ink. His novels, *My Apartment, Change*, and Broken Gopher Ink's *Collected Plays* and *Murder In The Men's Store* are available on Amazon.com and fine bookstores everywhere. A rockin' audio version of *Change* is available at audible.com.

Ali Shehzad Zaidi is a professor of English and Humanities at SUNY.

❧ *Chiron Review* Patrons ❧

Blue Horse Press

Alan Catlin

Alice Czalpinski

W.D. Ehrhart

Galusha

Roman Gladstone

Jay Griswold

Robert Headley

Max Mavis

Steve & Mary Sassmann

Dr. Patrick Stang

Marc Swan

Thespis & Minou

Ralph F. Voss
(1943-2021)

(21) Anonymous

❧ *Special Thanks* ❧

Putzina Press

Your support is vital.

Our issues back to #119 are at Amazon.com, B&N & Lulu.com.
Subscriptions are $49 for 1 year/4 issues. Donations are tax
deductible. Payment may be made via PayPal
(with this email address, chironreview2@gmail.com),
Venmo: @michael-hathaway-43,
or check, or money order payable to:
Chiron, Inc., 522 E. South Ave., St. John, KS 67576
chironreview.godaddysites.com